Not In The Eye

The story of the biggest event in porn history, and how a lone reporter influenced a million-dollar court case. Reproduced in part from the monthly articles by **Indigo Julius**, who can be found online, contributing monthly to *Words are Verbatim e-zine*.

Not In The Eye

C Z Hazard

To STUART,

THANKS FOR BACKING,

C Z H!

B*STAR KITTY PRESS
First Published Online in 2013
First Print Edition 2015

Published by B*Star Kitty Press

This edition funded by Kickstarter

For S by S

Chapter One

I missed the stop sign as I was flicking ash off of my $200 khakis, concerned about the possibility of another resin burn. Most of my clothes live on the floor immediately surrounding my suitcase, but I constantly tell people I have moths in my non-existent closet.

The cop car pulled out behind me, more light and sound than the Lady Gaga memorial concert that I was backstage at last week. I now had a choice: drive hard, dump the car and get my agent to 'phone it in as stolen, or pull over and risk finding the one cop in SoCal who wouldn't take a bribe.

I tried to drop the piranha into fourth gear, but it was another lazy-ass automatic [I miss Europe; I "test-drove" the new Ferrari for three weeks while I was out there, for an "article" on super-cars that never existed. It would have been a damn good article too, if the Italian for shark had translated better, and if I hadn't written off the supercar. You know, I would have written the damn piece, but it didn't pay well and it just felt so... passé. It's a shame I hadn't been hurt, as that would have made a worthwhile article. Mind you, if I'd been injured badly, well, I'd probably have *another* book deal to contend with. If I'd killed someone in the crash? Shit, I'd probably have my own TV show]. Silver trim and lining.

Still, this independent driving mechanism meant my free hand could operate my brand-new 2TB iPod that Stephen gave me for my birthday, as I selected the appropriate background music for the ensuing chase. I opted for track five from the forthcoming Neo-Nirvana album; you mere mortals will see it in the store in about three months' time.

It pays to be the biggest name in nu-Gonzo ™ media-journalism. All the bloggers may hate me, but that's only because I, **Indigo Julius**, refuse to do for pay what most would do for free, picking and choosing the best work. I have had more court cases taken out against me than *Private Eye*, all for breach of contract. I have even more injunctions preventing me from writing about certain things and certain people. Apparently my word counts for something, like the making or breaking of billion-dollar brands. Just as my seal of approval can revive your dying acting career or put your unheard-of band on the map, my exposés and hostile reviews can turn your name to mud, whoever you are. Indigo Julius speaks and millions listen. And Indigo Julius should know, because Indigo Julius has seen everything.

The only problem in having seen everything: Where do I take it from here?

Towards the end of the second decade of the 21ˢᵗ Century, there was a palpable feel in the air that everything that could be done had been done. Media had become an Ouroboros, but instead of eating itself it was eating its own shit. Literally. *Human Millipede 6* was the highest-grossing film of the summer and returned Nicholas Cage to Oscar-winning status.

There were no properties left to exploit; the comic industry had been strip-mined of all its good ideas, characters and creators, and had collapsed in on itself like a bad sink-hole; once a quarry has been emptied, you're out of business. Print media was more or less dead, with only two major national newspapers left and your average book price higher than a cinema ticket, since physical print now cost way more than digital reproduction. Not that anyone *bought* anything anymore; we just paid for the rights to view it for the brief moment in time when it might amuse us, or distract us from ourselves or from the person sleeping next to us.

But still we had to have more. More sequels. More hype. Bigger budgets. Release dates announced years in advance, a totally synthetic gold rush desperate to stake a claim on even the most inauspicious dates on the calendar. It was a science; everything had been quantified. The studios knew how to exploit the market; they had the algorithms that could tell you everything about a movie's success by looking at the cast, release date, budget, theme and the competition at the time – everything but whether it would be any *good*. Not that it mattered; making a good product had long been written off as an expensive luxury, as a non-essential part of the movie-making process.

In this barren landscape, people were yearning to see something new. Something different. Some... thing. Please, Indigo, *anything*.

And when it came, shooting onto film at twenty-nine miles an hour, in 3D, at a cinema near you, it made the world take notice.

My publisher was still sore about the Ferrari incident, and decided that I needed to write a book by way of compensation (and proved in court that I was contractually obligated to). What better subject matter was there?

I had driven to California in pursuit of the ultimate story. In the one area of the media where honest, hard-working men (Editor: surely people? Indigo: fuck off) still strove towards innovation. If I could just shake this damn cop car before he called a helicopter on me, or started shooting at me, I would get to write my piece about the only growth industry left in America: The Porn Industry.

Chapter Two

It's a huge estate, easily dwarfing the grounds of the White House, with a similar level of security, as I found when I tried to sneak in over the compound wall. His security detail roughed me over and didn't seem too impressed when Mark Man confirmed that we did indeed have an appointment.

As I sit, Mark Man is fixing me a drink. He has Coca-Cola on tap, directly shipped in every week. Not the cheap syrup rubbish you find in bars and movie theatres; this is direct from the source. Before they can or bottle it, they ship some here. If he wanted, he could afford champagne. I ask him, why Coke?

Mark Man: You know, man, I've tried it all. I've done it all. Snorted. Sucked. Fucked. Licked. Rubbed. Drunk. Eaten my favourite thing in the world to eat… and eaten food, my second favourite thing in the world to eat. There isn't a vice I haven't tried.

He says all this with incredible candour.

Mark Man: I've shaken them all, but this...

He holds up his freshly poured drink.

Mark Man: It's the only vice I can't shake. My wife says I'm a sucker for a trademark, and - if I was gonna have a coke addiction - it was always going to be the upper-case, trademarked variety.

Mark Man used to have it all. Then he got more. He reclines in his plush cushions and lazily sweeps his perfectly groomed hair back from his face.

Mark Man: I used to think if I lost my advertising business, I'd lose everything. There was a certain lifestyle I'd become accustomed to. There was definitely a lifestyle my wife had become accustomed to.

His wife, Demi Goddess, from the UK, the self-proclaimed "perfect woman". She made her fortune by appearing fully clothed in every lads' mag[1] going, and by appearing as the Page 3 model for three years in the biggest selling red-top newspaper in Britain without ever once exposing her famous chest. Her gimmick is elegantly simple: she never fully revealed herself. Her "porn" DVD is one of the biggest-selling in history and is infamous for showing no full frontal nudity. No lips, no bush, not even both nipples visible at the same time. No one is sure if she was even

---

[1]British slang for magazines oriented at younger male audiences who masturbate a lot

6

penetrated vaginally or simply faking it, and certainly it contains no anal or blow-jobs anywhere to be seen. The cum-shot happened, but after she'd left the room. In an age in which we have become used to getting what we want, when we want it, at the tips of our fingers, Demi has found the hidden ingredient to becoming a multi-millionairess show business performer; don't *give your audience what they want.*

I say all this not as mere exposition, but to make a point: even with you knowing all this, Mark Man's achievements make hers seem small.

Mark Man: At one point, at ComProp, we had our finger in everything: casting agencies, literary agencies, marketing, development, branding. We expanded too fast. Like everyone else, we borrowed and spent based on what we thought we had the potential to earn, not based on what we were actually earning.

This has since become known as the MC Hammer Effect; the ageing rapper/dancer/man with several silly looking music videos serves as a surprisingly perfect allegory for the collapse of the US economy.

Mark Man: We eventually scaled back to a single agency, and concentrated on what we knew best; marketing and branding. But it was too little too late. Too much toxic debt. I knew when we down-sized our days were numbered.

Indigo Julius: Is that when you had the idea?

Mark Man: No, that came to me towards the end. During the dark times.

**

John Thomas (no, really!) is sat at his desk. He says, as a writer, it's where he feels most comfortable. Obviously, as a writer myself, I am most comfortable on the floor, lent against the bed in a small crappy room, fighting to maintain an upright position without pushing the bed away from me, into the door of his leaking fridge.

John Thomas: Yes, it is my real name. And no, I've never worked in the porn industry.

John Thomas - I laugh every time - is a bitter man. One of the key copy-writing agents at ComProp during its last five years of trade. Every year, when business shrank, John took a smaller pay-check, as he was too chickenshit to look for another job.

John: No, it's not like that. I had faith in Mark Man, in the work we were doing at ComProp, I honestly believed things would get better.

Indigo: You knew him a long time, right? Like, before he changed his name?

John: Yeah, when we met he was Mark (unable to print for contractual reasons – editor. Fuck off, it's Petravitch – Indigo). Another grandson of another immigrant who came to make a name and fortune for himself, back when that was still possible in this country.

Now he's Mark Man. You know, he has actually sued people for printing his real name, or for referring to him as just Mark, sans man? He had a perfectly good name. I don't know why he'd change it.

Indigo: Why don't you change *your* name?

John: There's nothing wrong with my name. It's a good, strong, American name...

I swear if he'd used the word "hard" I would have pissed myself.

John: Some of us don't need to change our names; it's just another attempt to re-write the past. That's what he and his "Goddess" are so good at doing. For the record, her real name was Julia Smith. Hardly a name destined for greatness.

He's alluding of course, to what has brought me to his house, for this interview; the impending court case and the incessant conjecture it will bring with it. Neither of these men should be going on the record now, and do so against the advice of their respective lawyers. I lied to get the interviews, telling them both that the other had already agreed to tell their story, and neither could risk having their side go unheard. I do what I do best; I bait:

Indigo: When you say he rewrites the past?

John: I mean, we both know the real story. The proper sequence of events; how it actually went down.

**

I push more buttons and get more information.

Indigo: I saw John yesterday. He tells me it was all his idea. That he shared something with you in confidence and you stole it.

Mark Man: Let me tell you something about John; he's played it safe his entire life. I gave him a good job, and I guaranteed his income. When I couldn't even guarantee mine, I made sure he got paid. What did he lose when the business went under? Huh? Somewhere warm to check his emails and drink coffee? His flat? I was going to lose everything I had built: my home, my lifestyle, and my wife.

He gestures to her and she approaches, kissing him affectionately on the cheek.

Mark Man: A lady like this, she has certain expectations.   She's a class act.   I wouldn't expect her to stand by me if I couldn't provide for her.

Indigo: So are you saying that none of it was his idea?

He takes a second before answering, and – even then – it's not really an answer, it's a politician's answer.   Right there and then, I have a good idea of who is going to win this court case.

Mark Man: What separates normal people from writers?   When a normal person thinks of something, they have a choice: act on it or don't act on it.   When writers have an impulse, they have a choice: act on it or write about it.   I didn't fuck about; I acted on it.

He leans forward, encroaching a little into my personal space, but in a friendly, non-threatening way.

Mark Man: If it was John's idea, it would still be floating around in his head.   He talks the talk and fancies himself a writer, but I've never seen anything he's written.   Do you see any books with his name on them?   A TV show?   A film? Anything?

**

John: Of course he's going to claim it's his idea. Do you know how much he's worth because of it?

This was a tricky question. Mark Man had money before, and his wife was worth millions. His estimated net worth put him on the Forbes 500 list; during a time where most people's wealth was going down, his was going up.

John: It was the night he told me he was going to have to shut the company down, that it wasn't making any money. I'm not sure how it wasn't making money, as he could still afford to drive his Buggati Enron.

Indigo: Veyron

John: Yeah, the Veyron. You know what he calls that car now? They made him a special custom edition with a personalised plate.

I shake my head.

John: Bukkake Veyron. It actually says that on the plate. They *gave* him that. He could afford a fleet of them.

That's brilliant. Great advertising. I never wanted one before. I do now.

John: I'll tell you how it really was in the final year. Despite downsizing, our company was still paying out $500k a year in salaries. There was the MD, his PA, two executive directors, the secretary, chauffeur, two cleaners, and me. The staff peaked at twenty designers and copy-writers, all of whom had quit or been fired, and I had foolishly taken on some of the design work as well as creating all the campaigns and copy-writing.

Think about it; only one person doing the actual design and marketing work in an advertising company? Me. How much was my work worth? Half a mill? A cool million? And why was I paying other people's salaries? People who, as far as I could tell, had contributed nothing?

Indigo: So at what point did you tell him your idea? Was it a project you were working on? Some promotional work for a company?

John: This was a completely separate area from my paid work. I was never commissioned to write fiction while I was working at the agency.

I could mention the falsified safety record scandal ComProp had with Delta Airlines when he worked on their account, but I don't.

John: Mark takes me out to dinner, because we're friends, right? And that's what you do with your friends, yeah? No, he takes me out to tell me the company is folding. Mark, he's very good at *playing* friends. He even asks me what I'm going to do once the company shuts down. I tell him I'm going to go back to writing.

Each "friends" is spoken slightly more bitterly.

Indigo: Go back?

John: It's my first love. I've always been a writer.

Indigo: Anything published?

John: No, but that's not important. So anyway, I tell him this idea for a story I've had. It's a bit weird, but it's different, never been done before, completely original.

Indigo: And what did he say when you told him?

**

Mark Man: I said to him: "Okay, that's your setting. But where's the story?" He couldn't answer. He's about as much a writer as I am an advertiser.

He laughed.

**

John: He didn't say much. We just finished our drinks, said goodbye and went home.

Indigo: When did you find out about it?

John: The same time as everyone else did. When it went global. That thing took viral memes to a new level, it was like... an electronic STI.

Indigo: Like internet AIDS?

John: Exactly. Like internet AIDS. Haha, that's good. I like it.

Indigo: Did you confront him about it?

John: Yeah, I did.

Indigo: What did he say?

John: He laughed in my face and said if I wanted, I could write his autobiography for him.

**

Mark Man: That was a genuine offer. I was suddenly world famous, people wanted to know about me. I offered a friend a gig that would have paid quite well, and got him in print as a genuine professional author.

Indigo: What did he say?

**

John: I said, "It was my fucking idea. I'm a storyteller, not a biographer. And certainly not a fucking ghost writer." It's only an autobiography if you write it yourself, dumb bastard.

Indigo: Okay, well let's not get too side-tracked. Where did the idea come from?

John: I'm not sure. I used to have a friend who was a teuthologist...

Indigo: A what?

John: He was a biologist, specialising in squid and octopi. He used to tell me about his work, I guess it kind of infiltrated my consciousness, or something triggered some memory, and one thing led to another...

Indigo: To coin a phrase; are you a wanker?

John: What?

Indigo: Do you watch a lot of porn?

John: Oh, no. Not really, why?

Indigo: Just wondering what else you might have exposed yourself to, for an idea like that to germinate.

John: Where do any ideas come from? I just thought it would be a good idea for a story. It felt different. Unique. A story about a man making a lot of money by doing something completely new, completely different. Like how *Superman*[2] was completely unique in the thirties, before all the derivatives watered it down.

I try to force an analogy; the displacement of millions of Jews to a strange and foreign land of infinite possibility, compared to that of a man shooting his wad over porn stars. Although, the more I thought about it, each cumshot engendered the displacement of millions of potential people to a place where every man has been before, and each human is the sole sperm survivor of a doomed locale; if the analogy fits... Besides, both created entire genres from nothing, genres which would change and redefine a medium for years to cum (Surely come? – Editor. Fuck off – Indigo).

Indigo: Can you compare the two? I mean, Superman stands for something?

John: For what? Truth? Justice? The American way? This *is* the American way: plagiarism and litigation. It won't involve truth or justice until we get our day in court. All Superman stands for is the ideal; that in all of us there is something special.

---

[2] Created by Jerry Siegel and Joe Shuster

That regardless of race, age or creed, there is the potential for something truly unique in all of us.

Indigo: Like the ability to shoot thick, viscous, *jet black* cum over porn starlets' faces?

John: Yes. I'll put it another way. Why do we want to be special? To be genetically superior? To become Übermensch? Why, if not to spread your seed? What for, if not to get laid more?

Chapter Three

Mark Man: If it happened the way John said it did – and I'm not saying it did – isn't it a good thing that someone took this idea and did something with it? Rather than it sitting in a drawer?

Indigo: Of course.

Mark Man: You know how much tax I paid last year? How many people get paid off the back of what I do? I did something even the Governator couldn't do: I pulled California out of the red. I could have set up a PO Box in Switzerland to avoid tax, or moved to Monaco, but instead I gave something back.

This was actually true, at least in part.

Mark Man: Did he show you any proof that it was his idea?

Indigo: Well, I can't really say, as it might be used for evidence in the case.

Mark Man: Come on, between us.

Indigo: He showed me a document which had a rough breakdown of a story idea, about a man injecting ink into his testicles, to get a break in porn so he could get laid.

Mark Man: And?

Indigo: And what? That was it.

Mark Man: Any evidence of a date? When it was written?

Indigo: No, it was only about two pages.

Mark Man sits back in his seat.

Mark Man: That's because it's bullshit. Here's how it really happened...

**

John: We'll leave that one to the courts. How much evidence is needed? If I draw a picture of a man in a bat suit and call it Batman before anyone else in the world does; have I created Batman?

Indigo: What's with all the comic references?

John: I'm calling on modern day icons, mythic figures that we all know and recognise. That's how much this thing has grown.

Indigo: Are you sure you're not just a geek?

John: No, not at all. It was just a metaphor. Black semen? It's as instantly identifiable as Mickey Mouse, as Mario.

Indigo: So we're on the same page, we both recognise how big this has become. Tell me, if you'd got your idea out first in story form, do you think it would have changed things as much as this has?

John pauses, tentative.

John: I'm not sure. Probably? I guess it depends on the medium. You'll always get people looking to buy porn. How many people are willing to buy a book these days? Especially a book about funny coloured jizz?

Indigo: I'll let you know.

John: Off the record, if your book does well, do I get any residuals?

Indigo: No.

**

Mark Man: Here's how it really happened: My wife, she made all her money from porn – way before she met me – and she's always got off on the

21

idea of filming me fucking another woman. We talked about it for years, and eventually I used it as motivation to go back to the gym. One night, it happened. She brought a friend back, I fucked her, she filmed it. She's a talented girl, she's got a real eye for it, and she's just as suggestive behind the camera as she is in front of it. She's the real brains behind all this. I'm just the meat.

Demi: Ah, babe, how sweet.

She moves from her position behind the white sofa, where she's been stood massaging his shoulders, and leans over the sofa to kiss him. This is how they complement each other. This is affection. I pretend to check my notes while they progress to full-on petting. I briefly think I might end up seeing something you can't buy on DVD. I think they only stop because their fiscally aware subconscious has kicked in, telling them that I haven't paid anything to watch this display.

Mark Man: You see? Who could resist her? Well, anyway, we watched the home movie and it, uh, it looked good. You know? I looked good. I performed well. When the agency went under, she used her contacts, shopped the tape around. She tried to get me a gig.

Indigo: Any luck?

Mark Man: I got a scene or two. It's hard work, man; you've no idea of the pressure, and the timing. It's all about when everyone else is ready for you to cum, not when you're ready. It's weird.

Indigo: And then?

Mark Man: And then nothing. Apparently I was too average. Going to the gym was a waste of time; they said, with the way porn was, I would have been better off getting fat, or waiting until I was old, or deformed or scarred up, or lost a limb. If I'd been a midget, I'd have had a shot. Anything to give me an edge, to make me a freak, to degrade the woman more.

You remember when porn was just two people fucking?

Indigo: No.

I honestly don't.

Mark Man: Yeah, this ain't your parents' porn. I remember my Dad used to keep porn hidden under his shoe storage in his closet, so my brother and I couldn't find it. Now the roles are reversed: I keep porn I'm in hidden from my parents. Although, they probably wouldn't know what it is even if they saw it. Some of it is barely recognisable as porn.

Indigo: Fucked up.

Mark Man: Tell me about it. If I ever find my kid's porn stash, I'm gonna give it a wide berth. I hate to think what will pass for porn in his day.

Indigo: Kid?

Demi: I'm pregnant.

Mark Man: It's true, dude.

Indigo: Seriously? Congratulations.

Mark Man: We only found out yesterday.

Indigo: Oh, wow. Have you given me the exclusive?

Mark Man: No, our publicist already sold the announcement. I can't even remember who paid for it. Or how much.

Demi: A lot.

Found out yesterday, and they've already sold the exclusive before I could claim it. That, I could believe; they had sold their exclusive wedding photos for $250,000 to a glossy celeb mag, the first time they ever used the word "porn" on the cover of a prestigious gossip celebrity magazine. Demi had since become known as the "First Lady of Porn". Mark Man starts to rub her belly.

Mark Man: I love you, Goddess.

Demi: I love you, too, Mark Man.

Even she uses his full name. They start kissing again. I cough.

Mark Man: What was I saying?

Indigo: You were going to tell me how it happened.

Mark Man: Yeah. So I started thinking about branding, about marketing. It was my job for twenty years, I should know a thing or two about it. True, I employed the best in the world, so I didn't *have* to do anything, but when the company was grass-roots, it was me on my hands and knees doing the vacuum cleaning.

That's what he said, honest. I know it doesn't mean anything, and I can afford the good drugs like him to find out.

Mark Man: But I didn't have my employees; this was me on my own, with grass stains on my knees. I looked back at the successful campaigns I'd spearheaded. You remember the Powa-cell battery advert? With the hare?

He switches to a monotone.

Mark Man: 'Forever, and ever, and ever, and ever, and ever, and ever, and ever...' That was me.

Indigo: That was you? You're an asshole!

He laughs.

Mark Man: Yeah, I get that a lot.

As he laughs, Demi rubs his chest. I swear I see her tweak a nipple - his - to stop him laughing.

Mark Man: That was twenty years ago. So I looked at that campaign, at what worked. What I needed was a hook, an angle. A unique selling point and a signature all in one.

Not too much to ask.

Mark Man: How do you introduce something new into porn? It's all been done. I didn't think there was anything new to do, but I figured a signature always comes at the end, right? As a way of signing off.

He gradually slows down his speech, waiting for me to catch up to speed.

Mark Man: So does a cum shot. Signatures, right back to the days of William Shakespeare, have always been signed...

Indigo: ... with ink!

He puts his hand up for a high five, which I return. He turns it into a gesture which manages to say "you see how fucking obvious it is?". He smiles, the smuggest smile I've ever seen. I want to hit him and fuck him at the same time.

Demi: Your so smart.

Okay, she said "you're", but we both know if she had been writing, she wouldn't have known the difference.

Indigo: But that's still a big leap, from thinking about the deed to actually doing it.

Mark Man: Is it? Man, I've told you how I've lived my life, and we already had most of the equipment lying around, unused, from that brief "saline injected into your ballsack" craze that was doing the rounds a few years back.

I shouldn't be surprised that Mark Man and Demi had not only been into that, but that they'd got bored of it and written it off as too suburban once it made headlines.

Mark Man: Don't look at me like that, man. I didn't think you were a square. Everyone had those for the parties; how would it have looked if we didn't offer saline to our guests? What kind of hosts would we be?

Indigo: No, I'm just surprised that you had it and didn't offer it to me at the same time as you offered me a drink.

They both laugh.

Mark Man: You're okay, man, you're on the list. Babe...

He turns to his Goddess.

Mark Man: ... make sure Indigo gets an invite to the next party.

Shit, just a single hour at one of their parties could write my next book for me.

Mark Man: So I called my guy up, told him that I wanted some biological ink, no synthetic stuff. We've seen what happens when you fuck about with this shit. Remember that guy who got the saline solution wrong? Just used sea water.

He shakes his head, shudders involuntarily and makes a pained expression, while Demi just nods.

Indigo: I feel his pain.

Mark Man: Now remember, this is three in the morning on a Sunday. My dude rocks up an hour later, with some honest-to-god cephalopod ink.

He reads my expression.

Mark Man: Squid ink. I'll spell it for you: C. E. P. H...

I make my notes.

Mark Man: So I'm probably still a little high from the evening's festivities, and I can't wait to give it a go. So I grab all my kit and... Sorry, dude. I'm being rude.

He snaps me back to reality, I'm so engrossed in the story.

Mark Man: I still have the equipment. Come and look.

We get up, and I'm being led to a bedroom by the David Beckham of bukkake and his awesomely hot wife, to look at the equipment he used to inject octopus ink into his testicles. I love my job: I haven't smoked a joint for hours and I've barely noticed.

Mark Man: Here we are, dude. I set it up knowing you were coming.

The equipment is modest. A standard drip, a dirty-looking bag of ink, and a few disturbingly thick needles.

Mark Man: This is where the internet came in fucking handy, man. We'd messed about with the saline a bit; a couple of times I made my dick bigger for Demi, but the best use was the night me and the guys pumped our testicles up as big as we could get 'em.

Demi rubs his shoulders a comforting gesture, as though to convey that there is nothing wrong with the size of his junk. We've all seen his films, though...

Mark Man: Man, that was a funny night... Wyatt made his balls *huge,* dude, we seriously thought he was going to pop them! What we didn't know at the time was that it takes a few days for your system to re-absorb the saline. Now, you might know Wyatt? Wyatt Kent?

Indigo: Yeah, yeah. He's a Nascar driver.

Mark Man: Right, and he was driving the next day. You know that thing about racers? About how if they need to piss they just go in their suits? If a driver crashes he could burst his bladder, and he'd run the risk of poisoning his system before he could be cut free from the car.

Indigo: Oh, man.

Mark Man: Yeah, dude, yeah! If he'd crashed, his testicles would have exploded. You've never seen a slower Nascar.

Indigo: Fucked up!

Demi: You never told me about that!

Mark is laughing hysterically, and he eventually dismisses Demi's concern, rather flippantly; this is a normal sort of activity for him.

Mark Man: It's just me and the guys, messing about. Don't worry. Hey, Indigo, look for his post-race interview: you can see the bulge!

It's a funny visual, and I laugh along.

Mark Man: Oh, man. Funny shit. So, anyway. We needed to look this up on the internet to see what had to be done. I needed to go deep, deep into my testicles. I needed to know where to go; it was hardly an exact science. I was aiming for the 'Vas Deferens', which is where the mature sperm are stored immediately before ejaculation.

I did some research on this, and this is what Wikipedia has to say about it:

During ejaculation, the smooth muscle in the walls of the vas deferens contracts reflexively, thus propelling the sperm forward. This is also known as peristalsis. The sperm is transferred from the vas deferens into the urethra, collecting secretions from the male accessory sex glands such as the seminal vesicles, prostate gland and the bulbourethral glands, which form the bulk of semen.

Way to take all the fun out of it, huh? Remember all that, next time you're spaffing on some bird's tits.

Mark Man: It fucking hurt.

Indigo: And?

Mark Man: After a half hour or so, we tried to fuck. But it hurt, every time my balls bounced off her ass, it felt like someone was electrocuting my taint. Eventually – and I hasten to add it was the only time fucking Demi ever felt like a chore...

Demi: Aw.

Mark Man: ... eventually, I came. It was normal, exactly the same as every other time.

Indigo: Oh.

Mark Man: Yeah. Hashtag fail.

Indigo: Right.

Mark Man: So now I was just an idiot walking around with octopus ink floating around aimlessly in my junk. I figured, like the saline, my body would eventually absorb it. No harm, no foul.

Indigo: But it didn't?

Mark Man: No. I was in chronic pain for a few days, and my dick just started to itch. You know, like when you have an STI?

This is a trick question. Never answer this question. Stay neutral.

Mark Man: It's the kind of itch that you just need to scratch, and what's the best way to scratch your cock? Inevitably, at some point scratching becomes jacking off, right?

I shrug.

Indigo: Sure.

Demi: Yep.

Mark Man: The pleasure and the pain was an intense mix, like when you cut the head of your penis a tiny bit. I'd definitely recommend it. At the time I thought maybe I'd got an infection, but that didn't stop the wanking. Shit, if it was an infection, best to get as much wanking done now, before the possibility of losing the cock, right?

This made sense.

Mark Man: It was intoxicating. I couldn't stop. This wasn't a planned session. I didn't have my mankerchief at hand. I just thought I'd cum on the silk sheets, and - if Demi complained - I could always say it must've leaked out of her. I've done it before.

She hits him, playfully. Such a cute couple.

Mark Man: So I stood right here, wanking faster than I ever have before. I thought my arm was going to drop off. When I finally came, it almost went through the wall. It was a good job there wasn't a mouth around it; it could have shot your fucking tonsils off.

She smiles at him, looking oddly proud.

Mark Man: By the time I finished, I had stars in front of my eyes. I thought I might pass out. But, as my vision cleared, I realised some of the dots weren't from my vision. I had done it after all, succeeded. My cum was black!

Chapter Four

Mark Man: What I'd done, in my drunken haste, is I'd aimed for the wrong bit. Some of those internet diagrams are detailed, and I'm no doctor. I'd gone deep, much deeper than I actually needed to, and hit the epididymis, where the sperm mature. It took a few days, but – as the new sperm cells formed – they picked up colouration from the foreign ink deposit. I guess it doesn't matter how it happened, though.   I had done it.   I had my edge, my signature. I got Demi to book a second scene.

Demi: It took some doing, but they agreed.

Mark Man: Did you ever see the first video? It was rough, not many copies exist. No one knew it was coming: the director had no idea; the starlet didn't have a clue. *No one* knew what had just happened.

**

Derek Wang: It was like watching Jesus being born. You knew it was significant, but you couldn't say why.

Derek Wang is the director of the first video scene to feature Mark Man's infamous black cumshot.

Derek: He didn't tell any of us. I remember him walking into the studio, all swagger and balls. He looked like the kid at school who knew he was going to win show-and-tell. Forever.

**

Candy Cane: I wish he'd told me beforehand. I get that he wanted to surprise us all, but we didn't know what was happening. Apparently, I started freaking out.

Candy Cane. Probably the sixth "starlet" to use that name in the industry, in California alone. Nothing about her is original, neither in creative terms nor in body parts. She will go to the grave remembered as "that person who was the first person who got black cum in her face". They might have to use an acronym to fit it on the tombstone.

Candy Cane: I didn't know what to do. Or what it was, so I just screamed. I thought maybe he [Mark] was dying or something? The worst of it was, my boyfriend was on set watching, and he was ready to beat the shit out of him. He thought I was screaming because he'd hurt me or something.

**

Derek: Seriously, go back and check the tape. It's brilliant. She did not know what was happening. A genuine porn freak-out.

**

Mark Man: It was the cinematographer who chewed me out the most. I thought maybe I had gone too far, crossed some invisible line. It turned out he was just pissed because – had he known – he could have used different filters to pick up the black accents better. A true artist. The only reason I didn't tell anyone was because I had no idea how long it would stay in my system. The last thing you want to do is tell everyone you've got this amazing unique thing, and then show up and deliver just another porn shoot. It's not like I had any way of checking.

Indigo: You could have checked, by way of – you know – masturbating.

Mark Man: What good would that have done me? If I jacked off and my spunk was black, well, what if that was the last of it? The only way to check would be to keep checking. Logic dictates that if I keep doing that, eventually that situation would be the one sure fire way of getting it out of my system before the porn shoot. Best just to leave it in that unsure state of flux and hope it's alright on the night.

Indigo: Kind of a Catch-22, Occam's Razor, Shroedinger's… jizz?

**

Derek: I'll admit, I was the same as everyone else. Shocked and confused. But instinct must have taken over, because once the situation calmed down, I talked to Mark. I offered him another shoot almost immediately.

Indigo: Were you mad he hadn't told you?

Derek: A little bit, but he got the Ridley Scott "alien-bursting-through-the-chest" effect by not telling us what was really going on. I think if he'd told us we would have played it differently.

Indigo: Was that the point when you realised everything had changed?

Derek: No, that didn't come for a few days. I remember - it was the day before the second shoot - I was thinking about how we were going to film it, market it and distribute it. It seemed new enough, different enough - yet still within comfortable limits - to be saleable, but you never can tell with porn. But then I thought about some of that fucking European shit, you know the ones I mean?

Indigo: Like the one with the dude who ate his own seed?

Derek: Yeah, fuck him. We've all seen the scene, right. We've got this dude, good body, good dick. He knows how and when to fuck and keeps his yap shut, just shoots the scene. They obviously haven't paid the starlet for a cream-pie, so he pulls out and shoots over her cunt and stomach. It was a good scene, and a great finish. And then, before they can cut, he scoops up his own jizz and eats it.

Indigo: Yeah, I think I've seen it.

Derek: Yeah, no big deal right? Kids do this in high-school now, but this was 2003, no one fucking did that. It was faggot shit, everyone thought the guy was a homo, the camera guy/director starts ripping it out of the guy, even the chick looks disgusted. You know what I thought when I saw it?

Indigo: What?

Derek: That within two years, everyone would be doing it. That's how porn is: what's shocking the first time eventually becomes the norm. There was a time when anal was risqué; there was probably a time before that where blow-jobs were rare.

I'd arrived on set, at the shoot of Derek's new film. The one thing that people never tell you about porn, the thing no-one warns you about, is the smell. Nothing had been filmed yet that day, but the smell had entrenched itself into the very building. It's not that the actors aren't clean. It's that there are a lot of bodies, fucking, under lots of lights. Bodies create heat. Friction creates more heat. You don't sweat like that because you're an athlete pushing his body to the edge of physical performance - like everything else that happens during "making love" that you like to romanticise - it's a biological reaction.

Derek: I only did the two scenes with Mark Man. This was the one that changed everything. We were ready for it. Now, I enjoy making porn, it's the best job in the world. But it's still a job, and - as a director - there are only two occasions when you *love* shooting porn: The first day of a new movie, when it's all new and different, and there's even that element of "wow, you mean I get to watch people fucking all day *and* I get paid?" The second occasion is the final day of the shoot, when you're happy to be done and you don't want to even think about your next job until you have to. It's a lot like prison in that way…

Indigo: …you only do two days: the day you go in, and the day you get out.

Derek: And just like prison, the fucking becomes something you ignore. But this day, this was a special day, the day we shot *Balsamic glaze*. You could feel it, something palpable in the air. I actually looked forward to going to work that day.

Indigo: What did you do before you got into porn?

40

Derek: Insurance. I quit in the end because I got tired of watching people get fucked.

Hoho, you see what he did there?

Derek: If you could bottle the feeling we all had that day, you'd make a lot of money. This was history.

Indigo: Surely history had already been made?

He shakes his head.

Derek: If you're careful and think ahead, you can control history. I sat on the original; I knew we could do it better. So we could keep everyone quiet, we used exactly the same crew, and I promised them all a small residual.

**

Candy Cane: They bought me back for the second scene.

I was going to correct her, to point out that what she'd meant was "brought me back," but this is porn, so her wording is probably more accurate.

Candy Cane: I thought that was weird. I mean, once you've seen two people fuck, you're done. You don't need to see it again unless you're adding something new to the mix. I guess they wanted to keep a wrap on this. We kept the same crew as the previous set. Same clothes, background and décor. Everything the same, except this time, I knew what was cumming. (this again? – Ed. Fuck off – Indigo)

**

Derek: The scene itself was arbitrary; we knew once people heard about it everyone would skip to the end, but still, you have to go through the motions, right? Longest sex scene I ever shot. It seemed to go on for ages. I didn't care. Positions? Whatever. Story? Setting? Inciting incident? Whatever. Pointless sex, just leading to a cum-shot. It's probably not that different to all porn, but...

Indigo: It's like a metaphor for Western culture?

Derek: How do you mean?

Indigo: It's all about the climax, not the journey. We race through life at hundred miles an hour, and it's all about what we can get, who we can fuck, the money in the bank. The house, the car, the possessions. We rarely take a second to take in the scenery. And then one day we die.

Derek: What?

Indigo: It's like Hollywood movies. We don't care about the journey, we just want the pay-off. The twist. The resolution. The hero winning the day and getting the girl and it's all wrapped up in a neat package. We're the culture that gave you microwave meals. We could never invent something like tantric sex.

Derek: What the fuck is tantric sex? Boy, I don't know what the fuck you're talking about... Do you wanna hear how I shot my damn fuck movie or not?

Indigo: Sure.

I sit down and shut up. Maybe there is something to my theory. This isn't the guy to discuss it with.

Derek: Aw, man. It was a beautiful moment, and you've ruined it. So, yeah, he came black stuff on her tits. It was history. We filmed it.

Indigo: But the original has leaked since.

Derek: It exists, bootlegs mainly. Mostly it's the same, but her reaction is different. More honest. I kinda like the fact it leaked, it sort of adds to the mythology.

**

Indigo: Tell me how the day was.

She shrugs so nicely I have to make a note of it. Her tits are amazing.

Candy Cane: Yeah, it was a good day. Good paycheck. I knew it was coming. Mark wasn't too bad, he could have been more considerate.

Indigo: Considerate? How?

Candy Cane: When I asked him not to get it in my eyes or hair? Some guys are assholes, they go for it. He just went for it.

Indigo: How did it feel?

Candy Cane: It stung a bit, but we have eye drops…

Indigo: I meant taking part in the first ever black coloured cumshot? How did it feel to become a part of history?

She shrugs again. I might make a habit of asking her questions that demand apathetic responses, just to watch her shoulders bounce her tits about.

Candy Cane: Like a money shot. Wiping black off your face and tits is odd the first time, but you get over it. I ruined a towel though; that inky stuff stains.

Indigo: So, do you feel that you were a part of history? Some people say this was the defining moment of porn in the 21st century: the scene that took it into the mainstream.

There's that shrug again. It's amazing that someone who has had over five hundred dicks in her can have such innocent body language. It's probably part of her appeal.

Candy Cane: I don't know. I mean, my work rate increased, I got a lot of work. Then I hit twenty-one and the phone calls stopped coming. I guess it's cool, something to look back on now I'm old and past it.

**

After the interview, Derek is kind enough to show me around the set. His crew are hard at work setting up the lights. I never really thought about the set-up of a porn shoot before, which I guess is part of doing the job right. If you're watching a porn film and you go "oh wow, that's a really good bit of lighting", something has probably gone wrong.

Indigo: What film are you working on today?

Derek: It's a big budget parody flick. We started making them again now, thanks to Mark. This is a big one, it could be the company's magnum opus.

We have something special for the finale. Something that has never been done before.

Indigo: What is it?

Derek: You're staying for the day, right? You'll see later.

We nod along together for a few seconds. I must admit, I am intrigued.

Derek: So in this next scene, Thor and Loki have been cast down to Midgard – Earth – and, stricken of their powers by an angry Odin, they have to learn to co-operate and survive on this strange new world. That's when they encounter this hitch-hiking hottie, while they're cruising in a pick-up truck. Take a seat. Watch.

I sit down, as the final pieces come into place. I look around as he directs people into starting positions. The mayhem of this morning's set, which looked like the scene of a riot, has clicked into place in the last few minutes. This is a well-lubed machine. Derek calls action, and I watch as the toned, tanned Asgardians try to pick up an impossibly sexy blonde and coax her into their pick-up truck. She has a body that could seduce gods... which is exactly what she proceeds to do. The scene ends. Derek calls this a "pick-up scene", which I know – from my movie connections – in a normal film means a re-shoot of something that needed to be re-shot, or something that was to be added after principal photography. Derek explains his version of a pick-up shot as "anything where they're not fucking".

After the brief shoot, and once he has finished directing traffic, Derek and I get time to talk again.

Indigo: So, the film you put out. *Balsamic Glaze?* Are you proud to have worked on that film?

Derek: What? Are you kidding? The money we made on that was more than some countries' GDP. I'm very proud to have been part of that. Mark saved the industry.

Indigo: You think porn was in trouble?

He laughs.

Derek: Porn wasn't in any danger of dying out. People will always watch porn, no matter what. But Mark changed things. How would you define the legacy of what we did?

Indigo: Coloured cumshots?

Derek: No, that was the macguffin; that was how we achieved it. What we did, what Mark did, is he took porn back from the bedrooms. He gave us back our industry.

Indigo: Really?

Derek: Really. With the increased technology, and with the internet, the industry was slipping away from us. Who wanted to see two people getting paid to fuck, when you could watch real people fucking, for free? In their bedrooms on webcam. In the office, with their cell phones. Your buddy's girlfriend in the bath. You'd all become pornographers, every one of you a filmmaker, with smart phones that could shoot, edit and upload a scene, while we were still arguing over location shoots and union hours. Our industry was in trouble. Mark changed that.

Indigo: How did he influence that?

Derek: You need to understand that porn influences people; we've got an entire generation now who've been taught how to have sex by porn. The conversation about the birds and bees is a little different these days; a Dad talks to his son about that and his son might very well ask, "is that like interspecies erotica?" A girl doesn't get "the talk" on the morning of her wedding day any more, if that ever happened, because her and her friends read all about it in magazines at school and substituted fingers for dicks during sleep-overs. The internet became our ancient Greeks, teaching the next generation how to fuck.

Indigo: You mean pederasty, when the older generation takes a younger male, and teaches them the ways of love making.

He nods.

Derek: Yeah... by fucking them.

Indigo: Intercrurally.

Derek ignores this and moves on. I've done my research, even if he hasn't.

Derek: The internet taught us how to fuck. Nowadays, whether you like it or not; we all fuck like porn stars. Or at least, try to.

Indigo: So, by that argument, the internet gave us instant availability of porn, which taught the current generation how to fuck. Therefore porn is needed? Necessary, even.

Derek: Yes, but half of the porn on the internet is amateurs, and that brings us back to the problem.

Derek gestures around the studio, at the lights, the bad set, the props, the talent. Even the intangible, like the plot, had been in danger of disappearing.

Derek: They didn't need any of this anymore. They had another person – or even just themselves – and a camera. That was enough.

**

While they shoot the main scene inside, I sit outside with Atticus Bluewater. I never bothered to find out if that is his real name, people just make up crazy shit for names to try and sound interesting (You're kidding, right? – Ed).

Atticus has been writing porn for the last two years. Inside, Thor and Loki are trying to repair a bridge or something, so they can confront Odin. I'll confess to being hazy on the details. It must be the hottest day of the year so far, and we bond over a cigarette in the small, two foot by two foot, blue squared area designated okay for smokers, the only one in a mile radius. Smoking blockaded, but we could make fuck movies more or less anywhere. You've gotta love California.

Indigo: How did you get into porn?

Atticus: You know, I came to LA, did the comedy circuits. I wrote a few bits for other comedians, tried out for Leno. It never really went anywhere. What do you do when you're in LA, and you need money? I auditioned for porn.

Indigo: When you say auditioned?

Atticus: Yeah, on *that* side of the camera.

He gestures towards the studio, from which direction we can hear the mighty Mjolnir hammering away. I've met hundreds of writers over the years. You'll always find people who seem to think that if they look like their profession, they are more likely to get work. You don't need to be a stereotype, but some people seem to believe it helps. Atticus looks like a writer. Ever though he's only 5'9", he gives the illusion of height because he's so skinny. Glasses. Balding. Little soul patch under his bottom lip. You wouldn't cast him in front of the camera. Atticus shrugs.

Atticus: Like I said, I needed the money. I was taught to do things properly, so I sent in a full resume and a cover letter. Derek called me in for an interview.

Indigo: How did that go?

Atticus: Well, I'm here, aren't I?

Indigo: Derek told me there was a story.

Atticus: Yeah, I'm sure he did. Well, like I said, I thought I'd gone in for an interview for on-screen, as talent. So when the interviewer asked me to show her what I had, I stood up and dropped my pants. The poor girl only worked in the offices, she hadn't worked on set. Derek hired me on the spot, as a writer. He took one look at my dick and said if all of me was that funny, I could be an asset.

Indigo: So how much freedom do you get, as a porn writer?

Atticus: Quite a bit. It's fun, easy work. The closest I can compare it to is a *Star Trek* script.

Indigo: Really?

Atticus: Yeah. Check out the rough scripts on the internet. They deal with the set-up, put all the characters into the craziest situations they can, and then whenever they get to a tough bit, where they have to figure out how to get the characters out of it - the denouement - the writers would just write 'science bit'. Another guy would come in later and write in all the techno-babble, all the 'tachyon emissions' and what-not. With porn it's the same; set up, characters, 'sex bit'. Done.

He draws on his cigarette, and then throws it away.

Atticus: Yeah, it's real quick to write. But you get a chance to fuck about, put your little comedy flourishes on it.

Indigo: Like what?

Atticus: Like, why is Odin angry with them?

Indigo: I don't know.

Atticus: Well in this version, I made Odin a girl, and let's just say there's a reason she only has one eye.

**

We go back inside after someone comes to tell us they've stopped filming. We catch up with Derek, who tells us they're filming the final scene. They've been shooting for two weeks, and the prep work goes back further still. Atticus and Derek are discussing some of the finer plot points of the film. I really admire their work ethic, and as they make final preparations and adjustments, I stupidly drop what I think is a compliment.

Indigo: To watch you guys, to listen to you talk, with all your enthusiasm for this project, you both come across as real filmmakers.

They stare daggers at me. I feel their disappointment, like I've missed the whole point of what they're trying to teach me. Derek shakes his head and walks off. Atticus and I sit down.

Atticus: Derek can get a little sore, but he'll get over it. Just watch the final scene with me, and I'll explain.

This is it; the culmination of the work. One of the big differences between a fuck flick and a Hollywood film is that – due to the limited environments and long scenes – you can generally afford to shoot the film linearly. Atticus explains that, other than location shoots, this film has been shot in sequence, and to keep enthusiasm and morale high, they are shooting the climactic fuck scene last.

Atticus: We already shot the scenes of Asgard, so we have the final scene in the bag already. Our CG-wizards are touching that up as we speak. This last sex scene? This ties everything up, all our story threads. Thor and Loki have put their differences aside, and with the help of Friend Balder and the warriors three, they are going to, shall we say 'convince' Hela to show them the way back home.

The scene starts shooting, and it looks like a high-end period piece; the costumes, the settings, hell, even some of the acting isn't bad. Atticus whispers, explaining they did a walk-through earlier, and everyone knew how and when to hit their markers. He says with a scene with seven performers (Heimdall is watching, unmoving, in the background), the cameras need to trust everyone to hit their marks at the right times. The dialogue isn't great:

Hela: You'll never escape my domain.

Thor: Silence, foul wench. My brothers and I, we have ways to make you reveal your secrets.

And then the fucking begins. I've watched a lot of porn (as research, I mean. Okay, and in general). Fucking is fucking, and these guys certainly know their jobs – six actors working as one twelve-legged beast – but it always looks controlled, intentional. As they approach the end of the session, the actor playing Thor remarks:

Thor: See, my brothers: Heimdall is showing us the way home.

Atticus leans close to me.

Atticus: How well do you know your Norse mythology?

I make a so-so gesture with my hand.

Indigo: Marvel? Or real history?

Atticus: In order to go back home, to Asgard, you have to cross the rainbow bridge, but this was broken by Hela in act one, and only she holds the secret to repairing the bridge.

Thor: I see now, brothers! I know what must be done. Come, we can return home.

At that, Thor withdraws and ejaculates red cum over Hela's tits. For a second, I think it's blood, think that something has gone horribly wrong, but then I realise: I'm seeing something new. A different colour. Next it's Loki's turn. The trickster god pulls out of her asshole and positions himself over her. Hela is careful not to spill Thor's now-no-doubt-trademarked red colouration, as Loki adds his own contribution: green.

Atticus: We're the first company to use all these different colours in one scene. All the actors had the injections, and had to be checked for the last few weeks. If something goes wrong with one of them, it will ruin the scene. Fingers crossed.

Then the warriors three: Hogun with blue semen, Volstaggs' yellow and Fandrall with orange ejaculate. Balder adds violet, and then, seemingly from no-where, Heimdall steps forth to complete the spectrum with his final contribution. Indigo. No relation (I don't know, you're a bit of a cumstain. – Ed).

The seven colours catch the light and reflect the vibrant seeds, coalescing into a glorious whole as Hela - moaning ecstatically - rubs it into her flesh. I figure it out. I turn to Atticus. He grins.

Atticus: Rainbow bukkake! Shot in 3D.

**

We retire to Derek's studio at the end of the day, and - workaholic that he is - he starts looking at some of the shots, editing some of today's work

56

against previous footage, some with special effects. It looks like there was enough cum, and – with a few post-production special effects – Thor and Loki will finally make it back over the rainbow bridge.

Today has given me a much greater understanding of how a film is put together, and why this is all necessary. It's not that it couldn't be done at home; it's not that the lighting needs to be better, or that you need a script and a plot in order to tell a story. This is these people's jobs, goddamnit, and like any industry you're going to have the people at different levels: Some at the bottom of the barrel; doing the bare minimum to scrape by. You'll always have the originals; scared of change. The hellraisers; pushing forward, desperate to find something new and more extreme until they gain acceptance or someone dies. Then you have the people to whom, it isn't just a pay-check, but what they do for a living, and they're proud of it. They're professionals. True filmmakers. Anyone can film a fuck; these guys are in the business of making pornography.

I tell Derek about this minor epiphany. He nods.

Derek: This is why Mark Man was, and is, so important to us. He came up with something totally new and original, but he had the *respect* to go to the right people. He didn't just throw it up on the internet, he helped design it, market it and sell it.

And hell, what a pitch! Riding in and just producing something like that. Who could resist?

Indigo: So, is that his legacy? Working with the professionals?

Derek: Yes. No. Well, sort of. Mark Man's legacy, he gave us back our direction, our livelihoods. With this industry, everyone is so quick to take what they can, and then get out while they can with some sanity and youth remaining. But Mark Man? He *gave back* to porn.

Derek seemingly remembers something, and stops talking. He starts riffling around in his office, until he finds a sheet of paper which he thrusts at me.

Derek: Here you go!

Indigo: What is it?

I study the sheet. It looks like a diagram of the modified saline injection apparatus that Mark had shown me in his mansion.

Derek: It's not the original, of course. Mark had one of those and the office has the other.

I still can't make out what it is? It included a list, I recognised some names as squid ink, and I think tattoo inks.

Indigo: What office?

Derek: The Patent Office.

Everything clicks into place.

Derek: I told you Mark Man was a genius. This is what changed everything. He didn't just invent this. He patented the procedure.

Chapter Five

This is why the court case is going to be such a big deal. It's not for the glory. It's not for the fame. It isn't for money. It's for Pharaoh money. By patenting it, Mark Man secured himself full control over who could do the procedure – a right he has only granted to certain established porn studios – for an initial fee and a cut of the gross from every film. Talk about your money shot!

On one hand, we have John - a writer - who claims to have thought up the idea and mentioned it to Mark Man. On the other hand, we have Mark Man - a marketer - who not only allegedly stole the procedure, but claims to have invented and also actuated it, and then had the foresight to patent it.

At the time of writing, the case is finally going before the courts just one week from now. John Thomas (snicker) is allegedly seeking $100 million in damages and the original patent, as well as all rights and profits relating to – what he calls – the intellectual property.

As a student, I spent an entire semester on journalistic integrity, being lectured at about fair, balanced, and – above all else – unbiased reporting.

I have been warned by my editor that I could be held in contempt of court, if I give my opinion on this matter. Apparently, my readership reach is so broad that I could influence the outcome of the case.

But this isn't your grandparents' journalism. This is nu-Gonzo™. I'm **Indigo Julius**; whether you want my opinion or not, you're going to get it.

(Editor's note: the following sentences were deleted from the website's original article, and are printed here for the first time, unedited. The following fall-out resulted in Indigo refusing to write for our website until... (Text removed by Author. We can both play that game, it's in my contract to edit you, and I told you it should have been printed first time out the gate, you spineless shit. – Indigo))

I think Mark Man is a genius. I think Mark Man is a porn pilgrim. A cock crusader. A hardcore hajji. I also think Mark Man is an opportunist.

John Thomas (guffaw) is a man with brilliant ideas but no outlet, whose one brightly shining (albeit unlikely) creative vision was relegated to a dark, dank, desk drawer, where it could have spent the remainder of its years had a fervent capitalist not... well... capitalised on it.

From the evidence he showed me, and from the way he talked, I have no question in my mind that John had the original idea. But by that same logic, if I draw a picture of a car that can run on egg whites, have I invented the world's first albumen-powered automobile? Did da Vinci create a helicopter in 1480 when he drew an "aerial screw"? Or was it not until the early 20th century when helicopters actually flew that they could be said to have been truly "invented"?

Having said that; what is an idea worth? When does an idea become an opportunity? When does an opportunity become a franchise? And has Mark Man already filmed a picture called *The Aerial Screw*?

Ask yourself this: If the roles were reversed, what would Mark Man be suing John for?

Chapter Six

It took another three months for The Court Case to happen. The usual judicial wrangling prevented the case getting underway until every scrap of information had been accumulated, all for a meagre seven hundred dollars an hour plus expenses, until every dollar had been juiced out of the plaintiff and defendant alike.

My initial plan was to report on the court case daily, live from the scene, with updates on my blog, hyperlinking to a full monthly article (available exclusively through subscription in my column on my magazine's website), and wait for the inevitable book collection to happen.

Day one saw me held in contempt of court, and threatened with a thirty-day jail term, as you may have seen reported on the news at the time. I took exception to the ruling and stood up to the Judge and spoke my mind, only to incur his wrath further. My weak-ass editor threatened to have me removed from the magazine. I put in a claim for distress and loss of earnings resulting from that situation, but this was withdrawn on legal advice.

(Editor's note: The five-day term Indigo served only ended when – despite Indigo voiding his contractual obligations for the preceding three months – our "weak-ass" team appealed to the Judge, paid a fine and brokered his release, citing unreasonable hardships upon lack of earnings. The "legal advice" was a quite real threat from our owner to Indigo as to what might happen if he didn't stop fucking around.)

I was consequently unable to sit in on the case, which hampered my ability to convey the story to you as it unfolded. However, this may have been a blessing in disguise, as you no doubt all watched, read about and followed the court case at the time. The last thing you need is a dry retelling of an old story. What you need is the story behind the story, from the people most intrinsically involved.

For all the preparation work I did, for the waste of time, for the loss of earnings I suffered, and for the five days I spent in county jail, all I have to show for it is one amazing claim to fame in a perfect, delicious soundbite: I became the first person in US legal history to be held in contempt of court for "cultural Zeitgeist jury tampering by way of osmosis".

Brilliant.

**

Indigo: So how do you think the case went?

Mark Man: You know, I think it started very strong for me. I had a lot of proof the idea was mine. I had the patent. I'd had a believable journey of discovery. I had the videos...

Indigo: I heard the jury enjoyed those.

He laughs.

Mark Man: I think at least half of the jury had already seen those.

Indigo: I bet the Judge hadn't!

Mark Man: Of course not. He goes to parties with politicians and real movers and shakers. He'd only be into the weird shit.

Indigo: Haha, yeah. I'm sorry I missed it.

Mark Man: Dude, it was worth it. Seeing the face of thunder on the Judge when you said you had nothing *but* contempt? Priceless.

Indigo: Yeah. Best five-day vacation I've ever had. You know I got offered a second book deal off the back of that?

Mark Man: Good work. I spoke to your editor to get him to release you. He told me you'd fallen out after he stopped you from printing your opinion ahead of the court case.

Indigo: Uh, yeah.

Mark Man: Well, I want to tell you I think you really helped. The support and encouragement you gave me. It comforted me knowing that you'd be out their giving my side of the story to the people. That you believed it was my idea all along.

He's somewhat right, so I don't correct him.

Indigo: Um, thanks.

**

Indigo: What do you think counted against you?

John: I'm not sure. I don't think people know who I am?   In the opening line of questions they instantly discredited me.

Indigo: How?

John: I answered my profession as writer, and the defence made me add "unpublished".

Indigo: Ouch.

John: Yeah. No one likes an unpublished writer. I went instantly from being the wounded party, to being a leper claiming he invented Harry Potter.

Indigo: Yeah, you know I heard that actually happened.

John: Sure, that kind of thing always happens. Someone tried to sue Pixar for *Monsters Inc.*; claimed it was their idea that never saw print. Everyone wants a piece.

Indigo: You'll notice no-one sues when the first edition book which sells two thousand copies hits the shelves. They always wait until the billion-dollar movie franchise hits before wanting their slice.

He looks at me curiously. I stop speaking, realising I am digging a hole.

John: Anyway, Mark is the guy who is suddenly world famous and obscenely rich off because of this thing. I mean, he has his own perfume line. Not only that, but he's popular too! Usually, wealthy people have gotten where they are by stamping down everyone else. Not Mark. He made his money helping a lot of other people make money. He didn't step on anyone to get where he got to.

Indigo: Except you?

John: Except me. But no one believes it.

Indigo: Except me.

John: Yeah, and hey, I know in your profession you probably don't hear it, but I wanted to say thanks. Knowing you tried to be there for me, in court, telling my side of the story to all your readers. It really helped knowing I had someone on-side, you know?

This is getting uncomfortable, in an amusing way.

Indigo: No problem. Although, I should say, that never saw print in the end.

John: Did it not? Oh well, that's a shame. But the fact that you had the faith in me is enough, that you believed that the idea was not only mine, but that I could have been as successful with it as Mark was... Well, thank you.

Indigo: Um, yeah. No problem. (This is weak sauce. Show some conviction. – Ed)

John: I'm serious. Your acknowledgement that I had the idea, I think that really helped.

**

Indigo: At what point do you think opinion began to turn against you?

Mark Man: I made a mistake...

Indigo: Some people erroneously claim that my opinion – that John had the idea first – swayed the jury.

Mark Man: No, like you say, that was just hearsay. If he'd shown you the idea before I had patented it, and filmed a movie, then that might have helped. But someone happens to see evidence after the fact? Nah. I think that helped you and your career more than it hurt me and mine. More power to you.

Indigo: Thanks.

Mark Man: In the end, the biggest screw-up was from our side.

**

Indigo: So it was going well all of a sudden? What do you think started to sway them?

John: The jury's opinion started to shift.

Indigo: Yeah, but what made that happen?

John: A couple of things. The fact that Mark admitted to the conversation with me at dinner that time; that started to plant seeds in people's minds.

Indigo: Why do you think he admitted that?

71

John: I don't know. Maybe he thought he could bury his lie in a truth? Either way, that got him on the back foot, and that got him defensive. He said that I wouldn't have known what to do with the idea, anyway. I knew he couldn't resist a dig at me, and I hoped the jury would take it as something else.

Indigo: Is that when he made the mistake?

John: Yeah. You could sense it, an almost palpable shift. It felt like we needed one more thing and we could crack him.

Indigo: The nail in the coffin?

John: Yeah, it's just... well, we didn't expect Mark to be the one to hammer it in.

**

Mark Man: The problem with a team of lawyers, it means you might not speak to the same person twice. Or you'll think you've been dealing with the one guy, but it's actually been five or six different people answering emails. All lawyers are sort of the same, really. We brought in a new big-time lawyer. This guy was supposed to be the best of the best. He had a fresh approach to the case.

Indigo: The Mattel defence.

Mark Man: He decided to play the angle that, although the idea was John's, he'd told it to me when he was still in my employ, as a creative thinker.   He decided that we should play it as an idea we owned, created by an employee who had already been adequately compensated, in the form of his salary, which I had paid.

Indigo: How far into the case was this?

Mark Man: Three weeks in. We were getting huge press attention. But the sudden shift in the case's focus worked against us.

**

John: The Judge ruled that we were in court to settle who created the idea, not who owned the creative rights. So although the court ruled in my favour, there was no settlement.   We had to reconvene for a future court case at a later date.

Indigo: So now you could lay claim to being the inventor, but Mark owned the idea.

John: Pending a future trial.

Indigo: So you could claim the moral victory.

John: Yes, but you saw how I was living after the agency collapsed; a crappy bedsit with barely enough room to write, no TV, plywood furniture.

Indigo: So you were the inventor of a billion-dollar idea, but you were penniless.

John: Yes. It didn't help. My lawyers were already working on a suspended fee scheme, they were so optimistic of a big win.

Indigo: So where did that leave you?

John: Up shit creek without a paddle. Mark offered me a by-line on the videos, and even shipped some with my name on them, crediting me as "the inventor of Blackake". That was even worse, because now my name was attached, but with no remuneration.

Indigo: I notice you've stopped calling him Mark Man.

John: Well, what's he going to do? Another court case?

**

Mark Man: Naming John as a creator on the video was intended as a magnanimous gesture. He claimed in press it wasn't about the money, he just wanted the recognition for the idea, but when we credited him, it still wasn't enough.

**

Indigo: And it was legal?

John: Pending a future court case.

Indigo: So what was the next step?

John: Keep fighting. Drag it back into court again. The second court case went in and out within a month, and the Judge ruled against us.

Indigo: And the appeal?

John: That went in our favour, and gave us a brief financial reprieve. Although, the wording on the ruling was somewhat ambiguous.

Indigo: I have the transcript: "The panel from the Court of Appeals said Judge Anderson had abused his discretion with his ruling for Mark Man Inc., concluding that John Thomas' employment agreement could have, but did not necessarily, cover ideas as it did designs, processes, advertisements and formulae, which are all more readily identifiable as such."

**

Mark Man: "Could have". That was the key phrase. *Could have*. So we went back to court.

**

Indigo: And the fourth time?

John: I suppose it wouldn't have made any difference in the end. We kept going, but it felt like we were Sony dragging Michael Jacksons' corpse into court and asking him when the next two albums would be coming out. You can only turn an argument around so many times. We had no choice but to stay the course. I couldn't afford to pay the lawyers if the case fell apart, or pay any of the money from the third ruling back to Mark, as that had all gone back into the defence case. So we just had to keep moving forward.

Indigo: So at this point we're what? Just entering the tenth month?

John: Yes, and at that point I envied you your five days in jail rather than my nine months in court. That was when the fever pitch surrounding the court case was at its highest. It had turned into a debacle, a public spectacle.

Indigo: Was that when Trevor made himself known?

John: Yes.

Chapter Seven

Ten months in, we began to approach the winter of the case, and I feared that the story had grown equally cold. All the research, the interviews, and the commentary that I had prepared before the court case, the friendships I had forged, betrayed and re-forged; all looked to be for naught. What had begun as a simple investigative piece to satisfy a book deal contract (the retainer for which had long since been wasted) had inflated into the biggest story in the world, and then turned into the most boring, hackneyed court case, mired in drudgery and re-iteration. Like a balloon which had threatened to explode, catching the attention of party-goers mid-revel, it had then proceeded to deflate slowly, over a series of months, until it was a withered, wrinkly thing, ignored and left taped to the wall, a faded reminder of how interesting it had been for that brief moment in time. Balloons are intended to pop while they're still full of potential, not die a protracted, uninspiring death.

I'll admit I was worried: on the back of this court case and my temporary incarceration, I had signed an additional book deal, and now wondered if I had enough content even for just one. Without an ending, I was left in the same litigious limbo as John Thomas (chortle) and Mark Man.

Luckily, into this dark arena came an unlikely hero. A real all-American boy with a story to tell, and the perfect stage on which to sell it.

If my analogous nature wears thin, please bear with me. When I compare the American court system to an arena, when I describe Trevor Goodenough as a four-dimensional, larger than life character, I do so not for hyperbole's sake, but for good reason. If you don't believe me, read his book (available now from both good bookstores), he'll tell you all about it himself.

If you don't believe me, then answer me this: How many people have you seen enter a court room to their own entrance music?[3]

**

Indigo: For the benefit of any of my readers who might not already know you, take a second to describe yourself.

Trevor Goodenough: Why wouldn't they know me?

---

[3]The Coal Chamber version of "Shock the Monkey", for those keeping score

Indigo: Just for clarity's sake.

Trevor: If they don't know of me by now, they don't deserve to.

He laughs, and muscle memory has him mimicking an action akin to someone throwing trademark long, blond hair back over his head. Hair which had long since departed.

Trevor: What's to say? I've been a Pro-NFL'er, a Pro-Wrestler and a porn star. I've had three successful careers and I've been the top of the game with all three of them; that's one more than Arnie, when you count his Governorship. If you want to know more, buy my book.

That somewhat truncated version of his life story doesn't do him justice. A Kansas farm-boy, at eighteen he finished his college education on the back of a fully-paid football scholarship. He already had five NFL teams bidding for his attention. He made his first million before he'd ever played a professional game. Some people described him as the Shaquille O'Neal of pro-Football. He stands 6'5" and weighed, at his peak, 265 pounds. Although shorter than the NBA giant, and although far from his game-weight at the time of our meeting, he is still an imposing figure.

Indigo: Tell us a bit about your football career.

Trevor: What can I tell you? I took my high school, and then my college, to the top of their leagues. We won the Bowl Championship series, and I was awarded the Heisman Trophy. I was the highest paid rookie in the history of the game.

Indigo: Who made more money in college, you, or Shaq?

Trevor: Please? Adjusting for inflation or base-rate? Either way, it's me. You know Sports Trading Cards? Who do you think has the more expensive Rookie card?

This is not my field. He might as well have asked me who's the best Pokemon.

Indigo: You?

Trevor: No. Shaq. His card is much rarer. They made hundreds of thousands of cards for me, because everyone knew I was going to be the next big thing in pro-football, even as a rookie.

Indigo: So where did it go wrong?

Trevor: I'm not sure if it did? Sure, there were hiccups. Twists and turns in the road of life. But I kept moving forward. I've been very lucky.

Indigo: So what was the first "hiccup"?

Trevor: Before I even completed my first pro-season, I blew my knee out; tore some articular cartilage right off the bone.

Indigo: Ouch!

Trevor: Yeah. Ouch. It was in a game. I went to turn one way, my leg kept going the other way. No contact. No foul-play. No stupidity.

He shrugs

Trevor: Just one of those things.

**

Indigo: How did you feel when Trevor entered the court room?

He sighs massively, reclining in his chair. He sits, contemplating the answer. Mark Man is never at a loss for words, but for once, he seems to be really struggling to find the right soundbite to sum up that moment in time for him. A moment which had a massive effect at the key moment of a multi-million-dollar court case. He looked like he had found the words.

Mark Man: Fucked up, man...

**

Indigo: So with your pro-football career over, what was next?

Trevor: After a period of rehabilitation, mental and physical, I got a call-up from one of the nationwide wrestling companies.

Indigo: How did that affect your knee?

Trevor: Well, I'd had surgery. Autologous chondrocyte implantation is what they called it. There was another treatment they looked into which involved stem-cells, but it's still technically illegal.

Indigo: Could you not do it abroad?

Trevor: If it can't be done in America, it's not worth doing.

It wasn't ignorance, but blind patriotism, indoctrinated from birth, that made him believe it.

Indigo: But your knee is good enough to wrestle?

Trevor: Yeah, the surgery was a success. I mean, when it got really bad I could wear a knee brace, which I took to wearing all the time; if there are two things you try and protect in pro-wrestling, it's your knees and back.

Indigo: So what happened?

Trevor: What happened? I ruled, man! I got a call-up from the guys and I went down for an interview. We talked about wrestling. I'd done a little of the amateur style in high school, before the school asked me to concentrate on football, so I had a ground-game for grappling. More importantly, I had the look. The rest they taught me. They said I had the right aptitude.

Indigo: How long does it take to teach someone to wrestle?

Trevor: That's not an easy question. I've seen guys 'study' down in Ohio for years, and they've never gotten the call. I trained – hard – for three months before they put me on a house show.

Indigo: House show?

Trevor: Small venue, no television. They record it, but that's more as a study aid. Think of it as a full dress rehearsal.

Indigo: Did it go well?

He laughs.

Trevor: You've heard of me, right? I'm sat in front of you? I'd wager you heard about me before the court case, too.

I nod sheepishly.

Trevor: It's okay, I get it. You just want my take on events. I'll play along.

It's traditional for you to job your first match. That is to say, to lose. You come in on your back, you go out on your back. That's wrestling.

Indigo: And porn if you're a lady.

Trevor: Cute. I didn't want to lose my first match; I thought it might disappoint my collegiate fan base, and I wanted to make an impact from day one.

Indigo: So what happened? Did you fight your first match?

He raises an eyebrow.

Trevor: No, we talked it out beforehand, and we agreed that I would go over – you know? – win. Had they insisted I lost, of course I would have put my opponent over. I'm a professional and I respect anyone who steps in that ring enough to do my job.

Indigo: Fair enough.

Trevor: So I went out, did what we agreed, and I got a great reaction. It helped we were in my home town, so I got a huge pop[4]. Remember, this was before the dirt sheets on the internet hit it big and

---

[4] outstanding reaction

changed everything. Back then, people didn't know the results beforehand. They didn't know who'd been signed and for how much money. No one cared who hated who backstage, or who was shitting in the divas' luggage if they didn't receive sexual gratuities. It used to be about the wrestling, about the story.

Indigo: So if you knew you were going to win... it *is* fake, then?

Trevor: I'm not even going to dignify that with an answer.

He shifts uncomfortably in his seat, and then he leans forward aggressively.

Trevor: Listen, I've seen people break their necks, their collar-bones, their sternums and still finish the match. In football, you get injured, you get off the pitch. In boxing, you get knocked out, it's all over. In wrestling, that's not an option. You're live on TV, telling a story. You get injured – tough – you might still have five minutes to fill. So fill it.

I remain silent. Even post-chemo, this mild-mannered former farmhand can turn very intimidating, on a dime.

Trevor: You wanna know what fake is? Fake is collagen lips and silicon tits. Fake is the female gusher. Fake is being fluffed for ten minutes, while your co-star tries to make herself moist, with ten cameras aimed at her uterus. Fake is photoshopped DVD covers and Vaseline smeared on the lens. Fake is diving in soccer. Fake is match-rigging in boxing. Fake is steroids in baseball. Fake is the Tour-de-fucking-France. And I'm not talking about Lance Armstrong – he did what he felt he had to do to be the best – it's the entire sport that's broken.

He calms down.

Trevor: Compared to that, wrestling is *pure*. It combines everything: acting, athleticism, timing, skill, trust... And it's live. You only get one chance to do it right, and you have to do it right every time, otherwise someone gets hurt. If they didn't edit porno together the way they do, if they released a linear film of the entire shoot, no cuts, from one camera angle, everyone would be as bored as the actors before the final stroke.

Indigo: It seems to me, you don't really like pornography, so how did that happen? That's a big leap from wrestling.

Trevor: How did what happen? If you're going to ask, ask with your trademark question.

Indigo: Where did it all go wrong?

**

Indigo: So the court was finally starting to see things from your POV, and then Trevor comes in with his claim. What did you think?

John: What was I supposed to think? What little money I'd made had been sunk straight back into the courts, and the lawyers. It felt like purgatory. No one was really going to win the case, except the lawyers. I guess that's America: it doesn't matter if you're right; it only matters who can pay someone to defend the fact that you might be right the longest.

**

Trevor: I loved the wrestling, I really did. I never had much time for it as a kid, with the farm, and the football, but I always respected it. As far as silver medals go, it's a damn fine consolation prize for not being able to do what I trained for my entire teenage life.

Indigo: Still seems a leap, though.

He sighs, and shrugs.

Trevor: It is what it is. Wrestling was very good to me. It paid for my Mom's house. Mine, too. I even got my own action figure.

He points to a shelf on the wall, full of merchandise from his past life. He stands up and selects a figure from the collection.

Trevor: This is me. Before the gimmick. I was just plain old Trevor Goodenough, before they re-invented me.

The figure is a strange distortion of a man. More muscles than distinguishing features, it could be one of a hundred wrestlers. It's only vaguely recognisably as Trevor by the trademark long blond hair, which narrows it down to one of maybe twenty contemporary wrestlers.

Trevor: Somewhere along the way, wrestling changed. Or at least, the fans changed. Like I said, the internet has a lot to answer for. People suddenly had access to everything: not just our last match, but every match. The good and the bad, at hand, twenty-four/seven, and it's there forever. If the people have everything they want, including some of the crazy lucha-style, or the Japanese death matches, you have to give them more. We ran the risk of losing ratings and fans, so we gave them more.

Indigo: You changed the product?

Trevor: Only subtly. We turned it up to a notch. We took what we did best, and amplified it. And what we did best was characters.

Indigo: Characters?

Trevor: You have to understand, as professionals, we're out there wrestling four or even five nights a week, travelling hundreds of miles, trying to find time to eat properly and hit the gym. It didn't make sense for us to go out there night after night, killing ourselves, desperately always trying to top the previous show, raising the bar every night. We just turned up the absurdity. We *really* got into characters.

Indigo: Like who?

Trevor: Like, the Math Magician, Moonsault Sid, The Hurrican-Rani, Dark Henry, Russell Mania, Scooby Jew... oh, the list was endless. It didn't matter how offensive, only that it caught and held people's attention without us resorting to first-blood cage-of-death matches every night.

Indigo: Who were you?

Trevor: I went from the super-clean-cut baby-face[5], to wrestling with an off-the-rails, anything-goes porn star gimmick. I became Trevard Goodgirth.

He stands, and reaches for another figure on the shelf. This figure is more recognisable: the long-

---

[5] good guy

blond hair is greasy and slicked back; iconic skimpy shorts with arrows pointing to the crotch.

Trevor: My signature move was called the Vinegar Stroke.

Indigo: What did that entail?

Trevor: Do you know wrestling? Evidently not. I grabbed people round the head and I fell backwards, forcing the opponent's head face-first into the canvas, but I did a little pelvic thrust just before I dropped it, to make it mine. Smarks[6] online complained, said I was just giving myself the Rock Bottom.

Indigo: Could you show me the move?

Trevor: What? Actually do it to you?

I nod. He laughs at me.

Trevor: No. I'm not Kaufman-ing you, that's already been done. Twice. If you want a shot at infamy, come up with something original.

Indigo: How did your parents feel about the wrestling?

---

[6]clued-up wrestling fans

Trevor: They were real good about it. They got that I was playing a part, acting as a character. They were glad I wasn't using my real surname with the porn-star gimmick and all.

Indigo: How did you find it?

Trevor: Honestly? I loved it, man. I was reticent at first, but I trusted the company, I felt I owed a lot to them. Without them, I was just a washed-up, broken ex-footballer. With them, I was an internationally-known wrestler, a flash bastard who always got the girls and the money... It was a lot of fun. The most fun I'd had since college football. Wherever I went, people knew me and wanted my autograph. I had a song on an album which I sang, a duet with an auto-tuner. Great entrance music. An awesome image. People loved me backstage. It was a great locker room at that time. I could entertain, make people laugh. And I got paid for it.

He pauses.

Trevor: It was awesome.

Indigo: No regrets?

Trevor: None... I mean... a few. I saw a lot of people lose themselves in the gimmick. I really tried not to let that happen to me.

Indigo: What do you mean?

91

Trevor: It's like this: The Arizonian Diamondback had a hard-boy gimmick; he got stabbed to death outside a bar because he thought it was real; he never backed down from anyone because he believed he was a hard-man like his character. I did some work with a tag-team called The Body Fascists, who had honestly started to believe they were God's gift to women, and it nearly destroyed both their relationships. You market someone as the big superstar, tell them that they're the best in the world, without equal in their field, the works, advertise them as the reason to come to the show? Well, you can't be surprised when they start to believe it, demand a bigger fee, end up misguidedly thinking they really are the whole freaking show. A wheel that thinks it's the car.

Indigo: Did you ever lose yourself?

Trevor: Remember, I travelled the world. A lot of my peers, they had a different girl in every state, some in every city. It was easy. I wasn't like that. I had a girl who'd stayed with me since high-school; we were going to get married, but... Anyway, I never strayed, and it would have been so easy. I actually lost friends over it: the guys thought I was boring, or arrogant. I think they felt like I was judging them, because I knew these married men were cheating all the time, and I wasn't. I wasn't complicit in their guilt, so they couldn't trust me; the Serpico effect. The guys, they used to make fun of me because I was faithful and I didn't even have a ring on her finger.

Indigo: Why didn't you get married?

Trevor: I didn't want to do it just to stop them mocking me. I wanted it to mean something. To me. To us both. When the time was right.

Indigo: It had to be for you, not them?

Trevor: Exactly.

Indigo: So where did it go from there?

Trevor: I went to the top. Briefly. I was popular and – more importantly – a good worker. I had an injury problem, and we always figured it was only a matter of time before my knee gave out completely. I talked to the company and we figured if we were going to capitalise on my success, pull the trigger on a title reign, it had to be sooner rather than later. I got pushed to top card, and started a long feud with the Champion, "Buff" Lando.

Indigo: Him, I've heard of.

Trevor nods.

Trevor: Yeah, he's a decent guy. The idea was to push it all year, with me chasing the strap, and then, at the big end of year PPV, I would finally beat him. Be the champion. There is no greater honour than being asked to represent the company at that level. I said to myself, that would be the night I proposed to Marie, because the only way I could be happier than being the Champion would be getting married to my perfect lady.

Indigo: Wow, you really love her.

Trevor: Yeah, I even chose the ring.

I look at his finger. No ring. No tan line from a ring.

Indigo: So, what happened? The knee again?

Trevor: No, the knee held out. It's been fine for years, ironically. No, it was the PTA.

Indigo: The PTA?

Trevor: Yeah, the Parent Teacher Association. They took exception to what we were doing, because we had a large family fan base and we were doing some things which were deemed, "too extreme".

Indigo: Such as?

Trevor: A couple of our matches went a bit OTT, a few excessive blade-jobs[7], some cursing, and a few complaints from parents.

Indigo: What were the complaints about? Surely wrestling is supposed to be violent?

Trevor: To a point, yes. The thing that really did it, though, was the racism card. We had a tag team, a couple of young Asian guys. Indians. They were called the Hurrican-ranis, because they did a lot of hurricanranas, moonsaults, head-scissors... I mean, these guys were really good, progressive and talented, and we managed to package them in a way that appealed to our fans – a largely lower-income, white fan base – and we gave them a push. But we got racism complaints about it.

Indigo: What did that have to do with you?

Trevor: Directly? Nothing. Indirectly, everything. When you have a strong black role model, ex-bodybuilder for a champion, and you get racism complaints? Well, you can't really have him dethroned by a white, blond-haired, blue-eyed, Aryan looking Übermensch-type, can you? Especially not one with a porn star gimmick. It made sense to keep the flagship of the company in place, as a reflection of the views, of how seriously they took the complaints.

Indigo: So what happened?

---

[7] cutting oneself with a concealed razor blade to create the illusion of a hardway (a legitimate laceration sustained in the match)

Trevor: The big main event never happened. I jobbed out at an earlier show and got put back into mid-card stories. But the complaints never went away. They tried to arrange a compromise: they were going to re-package me with a different gimmick, but the damage had been done, and the network had gotten twitchy. I was only a wheel, and they had plenty of spares in the locker room. In the end, it made more sense for the company to fire me.

Indigo: Didn't that piss you off?

Trevor: No, not really. I mean, I was pissed off they had to do it, but I wasn't pissed off with the company for it. It was just the times. Better to put me on the sacrificial altar than the company losing a TV deal. That would have left a lot of friends out of work.

Indigo: Where did that leave you?

Trevor: Marie left me. I never even got the chance to propose. I don't know if that's a good thing or a bad thing. If she'd ended up staying with me when she didn't want to, out of some sense of failed obligation... that would have been bad.

Indigo: How did you not get pissed off?

Trevor: It was just one of those things. I figured something would come up, TV work or something. I did a guest spot on *Law and Order*, but that was it.

Indigo: And the porn offers?

Trevor: Oh, they came in straight away. I'd even had a few offers while I was in the company. Good offers too. Big money. Like, real movie money, not jizz movie money. Remember, this was before Mark Man made it mainstream.

Indigo: So you accepted the offers?

Trevor: Not immediately. I mean, my Mom was still alive. It was only after she died that I agreed to do a porno. At that point, who could it hurt? The money was much less than they'd originally offered, though. I guess the appeal had worn after I'd been out of the ring a while. By the time I agreed, I was barely an attraction, more an oddity. Another gimmick. A porn star pretending he's a wrestler pretending he's a porn star.

Indigo: How was it making the transition?

Trevor: Tough. The first film I did, I actually used a stunt cock, you believe that?

Indigo: Why?

Trevor: I don't know? Shame? Embarrassment? I'd only slept with one woman my entire life, remember, and that had been my high school sweetheart. I didn't want to get back on the saddle for a porno flick, you know what I mean. Once I'd done a few movies, though, it just felt silly using a stunt cock; you kinda get over that.

Indigo: Shame you didn't keep that up, right? If you had, things might have been different.

Trevor: I might still have my junk, you mean?

Indigo: Well… yeah.

He grins.

Trevor: Well, I'm afraid if you want to know about that, you'll have to read my book.

***From Unique to Eunuch: The Trevor Goodenough Story* from Pepard Publishing is available in all good bookstores for $17.99**

Chapter Eight

John: So in he walks, this massive, larger-than-life character. Huge biceps, flowing blond hair. Just a presence, you know? The room felt different with him in it. He didn't need the entrance music to mark his arrival, but it definitely caught the imagination of the media.

Indigo: Had you heard of Trevor Goodenough before?

John: I think I... yeah. Maybe. Caught one of his wrestling matches on TV at some point...

**

Mark Man: I thought the music was a genius touch. It made *me* take notice.

Indigo: Had you heard of him before?

Mark Man: No, never. But I'll never forget him.

**

Indigo: Okay, we'll come back to your lost genitalia later if you don't want to cover it now. Whose idea was the entrance music?

Trevor: My idea. It just felt like the right way to catch public attention.

Indigo: Weren't you afraid of being held in contempt of court?

Trevor: No, not really. I mean, when you got held in contempt, it did nothing but good things for your gimmick.

Indigo: Career, you mean. You're the guy living the gimmick, right?

Trevor: Yeah. Right.

**

Mark Man: The problem with his claim is this: I only patented the procedure, and it was the one-time rights to the procedure he was granted.

Indigo: Do you remember his original application?

Mark Man: No. My solicitors handle that side of things, but we don't grant the rights to everyone. Trevor had an influential director. If Trevor wants to point the finger of blame at someone, it should be him.

Indigo: Why is that?

Mark Man: Because ultimately the director is in control of the project and what happens in front of his cameras, and therefore he is responsible for his artists' work.

**

Indigo: Mark Man seems to think the blame rests at the feet of your director.

Trevor: What makes him say that?

Indigo: Something about him being in charge of the shoot, and everything that occurs on set during the duration.

Trevor: Yeah, my director tried to pass the buck too. He tried to pin the blame on the writer. He said it was his script.

Indigo: Do you think that's true?

Trevor: Where does it end? The writer will try to blame the producer who came up with the concept. The producer will try to blame the executive producer, who will in turn blame the marketing department for naming the film in the first place. It's all about culpability.

**

John: It's all about culpability.

Indigo: In what way?

John: Trevor is absolutely in the right. If it hadn't been for Mark Man making porn mainstream off the back of *Balsamic Glaze*, and then patenting and licensing out the procedure, Trevor would have never been in that position.

Indigo: But in the same way, if you'd never come up with the idea...

He sits forward quickly.

John: Let me stop you right there. I never would have done anything with it. Mark even said so, in court, under oath, that my idea would have just stayed in a drawer and rotted.

He relaxes.

John: The courts even agreed with him. Twice.

Indigo: Yeah, but on appeal, they agreed with you.

He tries to wave off his one judicial victory in all of this.

John: Water under the bridge.

Indigo: But I've seen the idea, you showed me it, in your house. You came up with the idea first, and if you hadn't told Mark, he never would have used it. You've said that, on multiple occasions.

John: Let me put it another way for you. Who created Batman?

Indigo: We went through this before, Bob Kane, was it?

John: Yeah, but most people know that, so don't feel too smug. But if you ask any serious comic book fan, you'll get a slightly different answer. They'll say Bob Kane *and* Bill Finger.

Indigo: Who's Bill Finger?

John: Exactly: Bill Finger expanded on the idea of Bob Kane's initial picture. He allegedly came up with the Bruce Wayne persona, the millionaire playboy angle, the Batcave, the Batmobile, Robin, co-created The Joker, and the whole origin and concept of the bereaved orphan.

Indigo: Allegedly.

John: Without Bill Finger's contribution, do you think we'd have the same iconic character? With the same lasting appeal?

Indigo: Who can say?

John: I'll say: without his input, Batman would have been another forgotten, flash-in-the-pan pulp hero, like Hourman or The Spider. The same principle applies here

**

Mark Man: He's a weasel.

**

John: Mark took a small idea and turned it into a worldwide phenomenon. My contribution? I drew a guy in a bat suit. And I was employed by him at the time, so it was work for hire.

Indigo: You've been arguing the exact opposite for ten months.

He shrugs.

John: I was wrong.

**

Mark Man: He's a weasel.

Indigo: Why do you say that?

Mark Man: The second someone else came along, and tried to sue us for the concept, he folded. I'm surprised he had the balls to sue me in the first place. He dropped the case.

**

John: I wasn't going to win. It was legal purgatory. At least actual between-heaven-and-hell purgatory doesn't cost you a shitload of money to exist in.

Indigo: Were you looking for an out? Or were you scared of the new claim.

John: I wasn't scared. I just felt bad, what had happened to the kid. I wouldn't wish that on anyone. I wasn't scared. I just figured, it would be easier for the kid to get compensation if the individual who was culpable was clearly identifiable.

**

Trevor: Bull. Shit.

Indigo: Bullshit?

Trevor: Bullshit. We didn't even get our claim in, we just declared our intent, and he folded. We hadn't named him in the suit. We'd only informed the courts we would be pursuing the inventor of the procedure for damages. He's a fucking coward.

**

Indigo: When you heard about the impending lawsuit, what looked set to be your second ongoing lawsuit, how did you feel? Did you ever consider conceding rights to John, making him the fall guy? Passing the buck, so to speak?

He laughs.

Mark Man: No. Fuck that; I was in the right. It was my idea, and I'd said so all along. My procedure, with all the good and bad that comes with it. If Trevor has some kind of beef with me, let him come, if you'll excuse the expression. He can sue. I won't back down or run away.

**

Trevor: Mark was a different story. He just smiled and said, "I'll see you in court."

Indigo: Do you think he was just glad that the legal wrangling with John was finally over?

Trevor: Maybe. But so far he's stuck to his guns. Whichever way the jury deliberation goes, you gotta respect that.

Indigo: Do you think it was fair of the Judge to impose a ban on your book?

Trevor: It was annoying, but for the sake of not impeding the trial, I guess it makes sense. I was pissed off when I heard Mark Man's book, *Discovery: Full Disclosure* would be allowed to go on sale before the case concluded.

Indigo: How come?

Trevor: Apparently, it wouldn't prejudice the case. All the wording he used made it clear that this was his "alleged version of events", whereas mine was sold as fact. Because it is. Also he snuck a question mark at the end of the book title, you can barely see it, as it's more or less the same colour as the background and you have to tilt it in correct light to see it. Clever, though. Shrewd bastard.

Indigo: Do you think he was shocked by the amount you took him to court for?

Trevor: What, everything? I think he was more pissed that it led to full disclosure of his assets, and an IRS freeze. It was his idea. It was the name of his book, after all.

Indigo: Have you read his book?

Trevor: No, I've got no interest in it.

Indigo: He "alleges" that, had you followed the procedure he patented, to the letter, you would still be...

I pause, trying to find the right words.

Trevor: A whole man?

Indigo: ... complete.

Trevor: Nah, that's bullshit. If he can collect the pay-checks for black cum, red cum, blue cum, rainbow cum, tartan cum... if he can charge my director for the rights to use his procedure in a movie called *Blacklight Bukkake*, he can damn well be responsible for the outcome.

Chapter Nine

The court case had been fierce, with all aspects of both men's private lives scrutinised. The media loved it; this was like a contemporary heroic fable. In one corner, you had the modern day mythological monster, the media mogul; Mark Man. In the other corner, you had the little guy, the people's champion, who had spent his entire life trying to do right by others, and – through strange twists and turns, through no fault of his own – found himself in a very unique position. Even for a porn star. Trevor Goodenough is the All-American farm boy, the high school hero, the collegiate champ. To borrow a four-colour metaphor from John Thomas (chortle!), Trevor is Captain America. But while Steve Rogers is a soldier without a war, Trevor is a porn star without a cock.

**

I go to Trevor's house, days before the verdict comes through. My last chance to get his version of events before the outcome.

Trevor: By the time this book is printed, all of this will be over, right?

Indigo: Absolutely. We're not putting this online, we're saving it until we go to print - once we have resolution from the courts. We've waited this long, we can wait a little longer.

Trevor: Okay, so I'm not breaking the law saying any of this. It can't affect the outcome of the case at this point. If I lose badly, I've been warned by my lawyer that I might not even be able to talk about this, that my book may get pulped. But if I speak now, before I sign a non-disclosure agreement, there is nothing they can do. So, fuck it.

He takes a deep breath. Silence hangs in the air. He has his eyes closed, and he looks like a man about to unburden himself. As a prompt, I ask my question:

Indigo: Where did it all go wrong?

Trevor: To me, this is just one of those random things: it happens; no one is really to blame. If it was up to me, I wouldn't even be suing Mark. However, I have lost my money-maker, and I still have to earn a living, and I did pay good money to use his procedure. A patent-protected procedure which turned out to be unsafe. So where did it go wrong?

He sighs.

Trevor: Like we were talking about before, with wrestling, porn had escalated, too. Even funny coloured cumshots were getting boring. Everyone had seen it. *Thor-Play*. *The Cunt for Red October*. *La Blue Lagoon*. People had seen it, and they wanted something new. Even the midget *Star Wars* porn parody; *Black Grape Yoda,* failed to make serious bank. The solution: we were going to be the first porno film ever to do a black light bukkake shot.

Indigo: What would that involve?

Trevor: The idea was we'd have a set, looking like Tron, as the big scene at the end of the film. Suddenly, all the lights would go out, leaving only the black lights, and all the guys and girls on set, the cast from all the other scenes, would use the blackout as an excuse to start groping, sucking and fucking each other in a mad orgy. We've all seen orgy movies before, and we needed a good finish. And what would be a bigger finish than a luminescent cumshot? Right?

Indigo: Right.

Trevor: All pearly white teeth, and glowing streams of jizz splashing over their tits, in their faces. It would look epic, right?

Indigo: Right.

Trevor: And dude, it looked fucking epic.   It looked so good, we made a few extra scenes for the 3D Blu-ray special edition, while I still had the funky jizz in my system. The plan was to release it six months after the theatrical and standard DVD release. A few one-on-one scenes with some of the more talented girls.

Indigo: Why so many?

Trevor: We agreed beforehand with Mark Man Inc., this would be the only black light porno made that year, to keep it special and to stop everyone else jumping on the bandwagon.

They knew, man. They say they didn't, but they fucking knew.

I give him a moment. I hope this is in some way cathartic for him, since it's the only release he has left. Eventually he continues.

Trevor: We just kept filming for about six days, getting as many money shots in as we could before the effect faded and it became too diluted in my normal cum. I think we shot about fifteen scenes in all. And man...

He actually laughs.

Trevor: … did my balls hurt after that.

I laugh with him.

Trevor: You know what it's like when you fuck a lot, and you get that deep ache? Try sixteen on camera cumshots in a week, and the amount of ball-banging that entails. I'm a professional, though, and – like with the wrestling – you expect to come out the other end feeling a little beat up. A week or so later, you feel back to normal.

Indigo: But you didn't.

Trevor: No. It kept getting worse.

**

Indigo: Do you think $150 million is a fair price?

Mark Man: For using a patented procedure and it going wrong? No. You have to look at total loss of earnings, potential to earn over a lifetime, interest, medical care, costs incurred. $150 million is too much. It's more than John wanted for the full intellectual rights and the profits of the global business.

Indigo: What about for losing your genitals? Your penis, and your testicles? Your ability to procreate and recreate? Continuing the family lineage? Is that worth $150 million?

Without hesitation, as if he's already thought of this on his own time, he shakes his head.

Mark Man: No. It's not enough.

**

Indigo: What did the doctors say?

Trevor: I didn't go to the doctors straight away.

Indigo: Why not?

Trevor: It seemed stupid. To go to the doctors and say, "Hello, I spent the other week fucking a bunch of hot porn stars, and my balls still really hurt." That's a good problem, you know, right?

Indigo: Yeah. #FirstWorldProblems.

Trevor: Exactly. "Oh no, my gold shoes are too tight. Pity me."

Indigo: Yeah, I get that.

Trevor: Or worse: "It might be that, before I fucked them, I injected luminous ink into my sack, so I could have black light cumshots. Could that be the problem?"

Indigo: But that was the problem.

Trevor: Yeah. That was the problem.

Indigo: Explain the problem.

Trevor: The problem is you can get different kinds of luminescence. There's fluorescent paint – both invisible and visible - which is what people commonly use for pictures, or décor in clubs, and in shit tattoos, because it reacts to black light and shows up. Then you can get phosphorescent paint, which absorbs surrounding light and can then glow in the dark for minutes, sometimes hours after exposure. I remember I had a toy car as a kid, it used to glow forever after I went to bed, and I was mesmerised by it. It was awesome. Maybe that's why I was so attracted to this idea…

Indigo: Yeah, I think I had an E.T. That glowed.

Trevor: Yeah, they were fun as a kid. There is a third type, though, which doesn't require exposure to light to keep its glow. Radioluminescent paint. The type they used to use in watches, and like they used for instrumentation in fighter planes during the Second World War.

Indigo: Yeah, I remember hearing the stories...

Trevor: About how they have radioactive qualities? Radium-226 was the most commonly used. I know quite a lot about it now. More than I did back then, which is a shame.

Indigo: Where the hell did you find radium paint?

Where the hell did he find radium paint? And why did he inject it into his ballsack? He shrugs.

Trevor: The internet. It was cheap. No one told me what to get so I just searched for stuff that glowed.

Indigo: My god.

Trevor: I didn't know, I didn't think. I checked with everyone on set: producer, director… They all seemed to think it was great. I should have guessed something was wrong; after filming, I went outside to chat to one of the girls while she smoked a cigarette, and she still had some cum in her hair which she'd missed with the towel, and we were both marvelling at how it still glowed in the night air.

Only in California could the night air be lit not by fireflies, but radioactive porn star cumshots.

Trevor: Like I said, I waited a few weeks. When I finally went to the doctors, it was too late. The radiation had actually eaten away a few of the more delicate parts of my testicles from the inside, so I was already sterile. Short of a stomach pump on one or two of the girls on set, I'd lost any chance I ever had of being a father.

Indigo: Jesus.

Trevor: By the time they took me to the hospital, they gave me a very clear choice: amputate or die. And I wasn't allowed to make the call. When I woke up, it had all gone. Balls completely, and most of my shaft.

He puts his head in his hands, and goes quiet. I have to struggle to hear him.

Trevor: For a while, I thought it was penance.

Indigo: Why?

He looks up, and it looks like he is fighting back tears.

Trevor: I'm a God-fearing man; I try and do the right thing.

Indigo: I'm sure God has better things to do than punish porn stars.

Trevor: No, it's not that. I'm at peace with that. I only did it for a job, and I've met some good people in the industry. I think God judges us by our own standards, and by my standards I've always been a good man. I only got into porn by chance, when all the other options looked to be gone. I pay taxes, I help my community. I contribute, and damn it...

He hits himself in the chest.

Trevor: ... I am a good person.

Indigo: Then why?

Trevor: Because the director wanted the final shot of the movie to be all the guys jizzing luminescent cum... but I wanted to be special. I was fed-up of being an also-ran, of getting screwed over all the time. I was bitter, for the first time in my life; I was angry and I wanted something to be mine. So I kicked up a fuss, made up some bullshit about it not making sense with the story, and – when that didn't work – I threatened to walk. I was the one with the special jizz; no one else had done the procedure and I refused to share. I'd already injected it. I wanted to be Tron.

I shrug.

Trevor: Don't you see? I was greedy. I was angry. By my own standards, I knew I was in the wrong. Pride. Envy. Lust. You shouldn't covet attention, and I wanted it all on me.

He starts to cry, and the façade falls away. I see why he needed the music in court. He needed the character. He needed Trevard Goodgirth to be strong. I let him cry. After a few minutes, he manages to say something between sniffles.

Trevor: It could have been much worse, I guess. If I hadn't argued, if they'd all injected, they all could have lost their manhoods. I did them a favour.

Menhood? No, he's right, manhoods. I push, one last time.

Indigo: One more question, Trevor. If you think this could be penance, if you think you brought it on yourself by being... covetous, how do you think money is going to improve things? Isn't that, well, greed?

He weeps, and he doesn't try to hide it.

Trevor: You don't get it.

Indigo: What don't I get?

Trevor: I told you earlier: I don't even want to sue Mark. But I have to, I've got nothing.

I don't get it, and I can barely understand him. He's a mess.

Trevor: Don't you see? I have to win. Otherwise when they sue me, they'll get nothing.

Indigo: Who? Who'll sue you? Who'll get nothing?

Trevor: All my co-stars. My Radium Girls.

Chapter Ten

In the nineteen-twenties, a group of women took their employer to court. They were suffering from a range of ailments, thought to have been brought on by their continual exposure to radium. Their jobs in the factory involved the day-to-day handling of radium, "while the owners and the scientists familiar with the effects of radium carefully avoided any exposure to it themselves". Indeed the company in question, US Radium Corporation "had even distributed literature to the medical community describing the injurious effects of radium". The girls, unaware of the danger of the material which they used to paint various dials, often used their tongues to improve the point on their camel hair paint brushes. Furthermore, it is believed that some of the girls painted their faces, teeth and nails with the glowing material. Presumably for fun. Many of the workers went on to suffer from anaemia and bone necrosis, which were worsened by continued exposure to X-rays in an attempt to diagnose an illness. In a bid to smear the girls in question, the company allegedly conspired to cover up the cause of some of the girls' deaths, citing instead syphilis and other degrading demises. It took two years for one of the workers to find a lawyer willing to go up against such a powerful company, but, when she did, five other girls joined the suit. This was almost one hundred years ago, and it was one of the most famous cases of its day, as the Radium Girls became headline news and media sensations. The girls won a settlement, and scored a major victory for the future of labour rights, and industrial safety standards were re-written as a direct result.

Radium paint was still used until the sixties, but, thanks to the establishment of occupational disease labour law and proper safety precautions, no further deaths or injuries were attributed to the material.

History repeats itself.

Whilst Trevor's "talent" had not been subjected to prolonged exposure to radium, they had still been exposed and were being checked out for any potential illnesses. Some of them had exceeded the acceptable levels for ingestion and were already suffering side effects. Thus the second generation of Radium Girls was born.

**

Faith: I don't know how to shoot a money shot and not swallow.

This is Faith, the main girl in the Blacklight Bukkake *feature. In the final scene, the camera pulls an extreme close-up, as the glow of the radium lights the scene from within her mouth, and then films her as she swallows the irradiated load.*

Faith: I mean, that's just the done thing, you know? Why waste the shot? We were doing something new. Porn has been doing the whole "watch closely to prove the girl has swallowed" for ages already, but we did it with a twist.

Indigo: Is that still a big deal?

Faith: No. A girl swallowing a load isn't strange in porn any more, or in a relationship even. But it still remains the standard: watch them swallow it down.

Indigo: Did you worry about any potential health hazards?

Faith: No. I mean, no more than the usual.

**

Akima: I've had a check-up since, but I had a pull-out finish, so I avoided the worst of it.

Indigo: At what point did you think there was something wrong?

Akima: I didn't. I just heard from some of the other girls who were having problems, and thought it best to have a check-up.

Indigo: All clear?

Akima: Well, they don't want to give me an all-clear, they want to keep an eye on it. Screen me for breast cancer, skin cancer, you know?

Indigo: I take it you're pretty relieved?

Akima: Yeah, I mean, this isn't even my full-time job, so it would suck if this messes me up. I'm doing this to get through film school.

Indigo: Do you not worry about your reputation?

Akima: No. I mean, fuck what people think, you know? Porn is safer than stripping, definitely safer than prostitution. Better for the economy, too.

Indigo: Any regrets?

Akima: No.

She pauses.

Akima: Well... I probably shouldn't have rubbed it into my boobs.

**

Harmony: You know why they call it a cream-pie surprise?

Indigo: No.

Harmony: Because the girls aren't supposed to know about it. We're supposed to act like we don't know it's going to happen.

Harmony is being screened on a monthly basis for cervical cancer. She took the only vaginal cumshot of the shoot.

Harmony: That's what pisses me off the most: the acting stupid, and surprised. Shit, we have more power than the men on set, and nothing happens without our consent. If you do something in porn that you later regret; tough shit. You shouldn't have consented and you shouldn't have taken the pay-check.

Indigo: So, no regrets on doing the shoot, then?

Harmony: No, and even if I did, what am I going to do. Sue? You can clearly hear me on screen saying, 'Cum in me.' Better that than pretending to be stupid, pretending to be debased. You get lots of people asking, 'Don't you find porn degrading?'. No, because I can be in charge. I find marriage degrading. I find advertising degrading. I find most media degrading.

Indigo: Why?

Harmony: 'Cause it's full of misogynistic bullshit.

She's a feminist.

Harmony: And don't call me a fucking feminist in your write-up! You should be pissed off with things, too.

Indigo: Why?

Harmony: Because of every advert on TV ever: full of misandry. "Hey lady, buy this, because your husband is shit and it might fill the hole in your life for a few seconds."

Indigo: So you don't consider yourself a feminist, then?

Harmony: Fuck, no! It's not feminists I hate, it's most women. Hell; most *people*. These fuckers are supposed to be my peers? I'm a misanthrope.

Indigo: I was going to ask you a few questions about the shoot...

Harmony: Films and television series tell us women are shit. Adverts tell us men are shit. If you listen to both you have two choices: Buy everything on TV that you see advertised and don't think about anything, or the mutual hatred of both genders. The second is the only logical outcome. Despite all its problems, porn is the only honest form of media left, because it's only selling itself. Not a product. Not an ideal. Just fucking.

Indigo: Is that why you do it?

Harmony: Yeah, and because I *like* fucking. It pays well, too. And I do porn, because I want to show that women can be in charge. Watch my videos: *I* do the fucking. But there I go, forcing my own agenda onto what we do.

Indigo: So – and I really did want to ask you some questions about Trevor and the case – you want to prove that women can be in control?

Harmony: Sort of... Look, have you ever seen those backroom casting call videos?

Indigo: No.

Harmony: They were real big business around 2010. The whole idea was a guy *pretends* to be a casting agent so he can film himself fucking some young, dumb cunt. Who in turn *pretends* to not realise he isn't a real casting agent.

Indigo: The operative word being "pretends".

Harmony: Exactly, it takes its cues from what should be a niche market. Essentially, you're watching rape by consent. That's why guys get off on it. It was a loophole to get away with selling hardcore rape in films.

Indigo: And you don't agree with that?

Harmony: I don't agree with the pretence that women are that dumb. Because we are not; we all got paid. You want to know what dumb is? This one guy moved to LA, and thought this would be a good way of getting laid. He thought the casting call videos were real. So he started doing it himself, meeting women and promising them a job, fucking them and putting the videos on the internet.

Indigo: What happened to him?

Harmony: They found bits of him across the desert. So you tell me who's stupid? The girl who takes a pay-check? Or the dick who thought it was real?

**

Echo: Is Julius your real name?

Indigo: Uh, yes.

Echo: Awesome. Both our names are from the phonetic alphabet, although Julius is from the German.

Indigo: What's that?

Echo: You know: Alpha, Bravo, Charlie, Delta, Echo...

Indigo: Oh, right.

**

Kayleigh: We should have known something was wrong when my hair was glowing.

Kayleigh was the girl Trevor mentioned earlier: the first tell-tale sign that something was not quite right.

Kayleigh: I mean, black light effects should need black lights to work, right?

Indigo: Any health problems?

Kayleigh: None.   I was one of the lucky ones.   I mean, we'll keep an eye on it.   But one day at a time.

Indigo: So you have to have regular health checks?

Kayleigh: Yeah, every two weeks.   I'm just glad, all in all.   I mean, I took a facial and I said to Trevor beforehand, "Try not to get it in my eyes," because I wear contact lenses.   He's a real gentleman; he aimed high, that's how I ended up with it in my hair.   When I think about some of the other guys I've worked with, some of the assholes, they would have aimed for my eyes.   I could have been blinded.

**

Indigo: Most of the other girls, they seem reticent to discuss Trevor. Why is that?

Echo: What's to discuss? Foxtrot, Golf, Hotel...

Indigo: How do you feel about him? Are you all going to sue?

Echo: Sue for what? Indigo, Juliet, Kilo... Oh wait, that's not right; it's India, not Indigo.

Indigo: Sue for the fact that he potentially exposed you to hazardous material.

Echo: No, that's *why* we'd sue. Not *what* we'd sue for. Kilo, Lima, Mike...

Indigo: Now I'm not sure what *you* mean?

Echo: He has nothing. If he still had the money he made from his wrestling career, do you think he'd be doing porn? What's next? November, Oscar, Papa, Quebec – I prefer Queen...

Indigo: Where did all the money go?

Echo: I've no idea. Romeo, Sierra...

**

Faith: Oh, the phonetic alphabet thing, that's a nervous tick. You must've been asking her questions she didn't want to answer.

Indigo: Oh, right. I thought she was retarded.

Faith: No, she's a genius. She's fifteen IQ points ahead of Einstein and Hawking, but still five points behind James Woods.

Indigo: She mentioned Trevor has no money, which is why you won't sue him.

Faith: Well, it's true he has no money, but that's not why we won't sue him.

Indigo: Why won't you sue him?

She shrugs.

Faith: He hasn't done anything wrong?

Indigo: How can you say that?

Faith: What? We all made a film with him, and things went wrong. He did everything right, called us all up to tell us what had happened, visited, arranged hospital appointments, offered to come with us.

Indigo: Guilty conscious?

Faith: Undoubtedly, but that's not a pejorative in and of itself. That shows moral conviction. Bad people can ignore these things.

Indigo: What will you do if you find out you are ill because of this?

Faith: I'm not sure, but I can tell you this: Trevor will be the first person I'll ring. And not to cast blame.

**

Akima: That's something we have to live with, every day. But it's not that big a deal. We're used to it. Do you know how often we have check-ups for STI's? Twice a week, if we're working. Any disease can spread 'round our industry in real quick time, and we have to keep on top of that.

Indigo: So you're okay with it?

Akima: You can't worry about it... sit around waiting for the 'phone to ring; you have to get on with stuff.

**

Kayleigh: Trevor would be the first person I'd ring, if I got the call.

Indigo: Faith said the same thing.

Kayleigh: Faith?

Indigo: From the shoot?

Kayleigh: Oh, Becky? Sorry, you used her stage name.

Indigo: Why would you ring him?

Kayleigh: Because he's there for us, he'll do anything he can to help us. He's a man of conviction.

**

Harmony: You want a cream pie surprise, okay, I'll give you one. So I get a phone call from the hospital the other day, to come in and talk about some results. Straight away, we know that's not a good scene. So I go in and sit down, and they tell me I have stage one cervical cancer. Surprise!

**

Echo: I know the Western Union alphabet too, but it is pretty boring, although the two identical letters are pertinent. Tango, Uniform...

Indigo: What if he had money?

Echo: We wouldn't sue him, anyway.

Indigo: Why not?

She shrugs.

Echo: He asked us to?

Indigo: He asked you to?

Echo: "Is there an Echo in here?"

She puts her hand up sheepishly, like a kid.

Echo: Seriously though, he told us we should all seek legal advice and sue him.

Indigo: I thought he had no money.

Echo: He doesn't, but he's working on that.

Indigo: Does that mean, if he wins, you'll sue him?

Echo: Who knows? Maybe. Whiskey, Yankee, Zulu. There.

Indigo: You left some letters out.

Echo: Not really. I've had enough X-rays recently thank you, and we're still waiting to hear back about the other thing.

**

Indigo: So, you know you have cancer; you have a real good case. Are you going to sue him?

Harmony: Trevor? No.

Indigo: Why not? You'd win? From what I hear, he wants you guys to sue him. That's why he's suing Mark Man.

Harmony: I just don't think we'll need to.

Chapter Eleven

As I write this, we are awaiting the return of the jury in the case of Trevor Goodenough Vs. Mark Man Inc. The jurors have been deliberating for weeks. Thankfully, with John Thomas pulling out (oh my god, that is fantastic!), things moved ahead much quicker than had both cases been in court simultaneously. I have used this time to get a final thought from our three contenders, before the verdict comes through.

**

Mark Man: I don't know why they're suing me. The entire production team is at fault. Hell, they're even profiteering off of this. They repackaged the DVD with a *Radium Girls* cover after it hit the news. They're just waiting for someone to die, so they can sell it as "snuff, after the fact".

Indigo: This hasn't been your only court case, has it? Your wife recently divorced you, and according to a pre-nuptial agreement – the authenticity of which was subject to much discussion – she took you for pretty much everything.

Mark Man: Yeah, I didn't expect that.

Indigo: I thought she was your rock?

Mark Man: So did I.

Indigo: All's fair in love and porn, huh?

Mark just smiled, like he knew something I didn't.

Indigo: So that's a case you lost. Do you think you'll win this case?

Mark Man: In this world? Who knows?

**

Indigo: Anything to add?

Trevor: Not really. Just that I'm sorry for what happened.

Indigo: Do you think you'll win?

Trevor: I don't know. I hope we do.

**

John: What they were doing swallowing it was anyone's guess. You make your cum luminescent so you can see it on them, not in them, right? Stupid bitches. But porn has certain indoctrination and girls get used to doing it their way.

Indigo: You're hardly an impartial observer, but try and be objective: Who do you think will win?

John: Mark.

Indigo: Who do you think *should* win?

John: Trevor.

Chapter Twelve

I watched the court coverage on TV, hardly the live, nu-Gonzo™ journalism I promised in the opening chapter. What started as a small article blossomed into a potentially career-making slow-motion tsunami, and I had been cast adrift on currents beyond my control, borne far from the seismic epicentre of the great wave, blah, blah, blah...

The thing about court cases is – no matter how you dress them up, and how important they may be – the fact remains they are boring as fuck. There's no theatre to it, no countdown. Where is the *Who wants to be a Millionaire* tension theme? They should use members of the *X-Factor* team to train each juror how to dress up a reveal. No awkward waiting, no drawn-out hyperbole of the kind I am currently attempting.

A lone, miserable-looking man with middle-age spread walked out with the jury. As they seated themselves, he read to the court, that in the case of Trevor Goodenough Vs Mark Man Inc., they found in favour of Trevor Goodenough.

No fanfare, no balloons, but some cheering.

He'd won.

It would take a few days for the full realisation of what that meant for everyone involved to sink in, and I knew the decent thing to do was wait a respectful interval before ringing people and harassing them for sound-bites.

I rang Trevor that night, but his 'phone was busy. It was a few days before I finally caught up with him.

**

Indigo: Four days have passed since the jury found in your favour. What has this result meant to you?

Trevor: Dude, it means everything. It's not about the money, or the security. It's about setting things straight.

**

Indigo: What has this loss meant to you?

Mark Man: Honestly? It's a pretty big hit. It's wiped out most of my remaining assets, all the money is gone after the divorce. I only had about $65 million in total once they sold everything off, the courts settled for that.

Indigo: Are you going to appeal?

Mark Man: You know, my lawyers think we should. But I'm kind of done with it. This has been one long, boring year. And you probably want to get your book released.

Indigo: When do you think the case went wrong for you?

Mark Man: When they heard the facts. I think the jury made the right decision.

**

Indigo: Apparently, Mark Man isn't going to contest this win.

Trevor: I know. He rang me on the night to congratulate me. That's really good, because it means I don't have to hang onto the money, just in case of an appeal. I can use it.

Indigo: What do you plan to do with the money? Reconstructive surgery? Start your own porn empire like Mark Man? Your own wrestling company?

He laughs.

Trevor: No, nothing like that. The money is all earmarked already, I'm afraid.

Indigo: What do you mean, "earmarked"?

Trevor: After I won, I got the girls 'round the next day. We sat down and figured out the fairest way to divide up the money, depending on who was the worst off financially, who had the most dependants, who had the biggest struggle ahead of them.

Indigo: What, with lawyers present?

Trevor: No. Just us.

No justice, just us.

Trevor: What's the point in getting lawyers involved? They'll just turn us against each other and make us think we each deserve more. By the time we finish arguing, a quarter of the money will have disappeared into legal fees.

Indigo: What if one of them comes after you in the future?

He shrugs, as is his custom.

Trevor: We all drew up a declaration, dividing the money, and we all signed it. We even agreed to store some excess in a separate account, a trust, should one of us need it in the future. How much do you need at any one time?

Indigo: You must have some legal recourse? Most lawyers would say that declaration is useless. The problem with having faith in a group is it only takes one bad apple...

Trevor: Yeah, but it's a good barrel. And that's why we've called it a trust.

**

Indigo: Summarise the case, how do you feel?

Harmony: It was nice to not have to fight for it. This will help.

Faith: Call me Becky. I think the result was fair.

Echo: Victor! Supererogatory.

Akima: The right man won.

Kayleigh: It gives me hope for the future, and better medical care, if the worst happens.

John Thomas: I'm just glad Mark Man lost everything. He's a damn thief and a liar!

**

Indigo: And what do you think the future of porn will be?

Harmony: I dread to think.

**

Indigo: What do you think the future of porn will be?

John: I don't know, I guess it'll get more and more bizarre. I have an idea for a story set in the world of porn, though, that might be cathartic. It's about a digitally transmitted STI, I'm calling the story *Internet AIDS*.

I nod and agree. It was only as I sat writing up my notes that I realised that, hey, that was my idea!

**

Indigo: And what do you think the future of porn will be?

Kayleigh: I don't know, but I'm out.

Kayleigh and Trevor have become an item since the court case. I don't know if it happened because of the money or in spite of it. At a guess, I'd say the money was beside the point. If I've learned anything about Trevor, it's that he commands loyalty. No, that's not right; he's earned loyalty.

Trevor: The future of porn? It's going to have to go really boring for a few years. Like wrestling. You can't keep re-inventing the wheel. You can't top yourself every week. Eventually you reach a

146

point where it's like, "where do we go from here?".
You either stop and take a few steps backward, or
you keep pushing and someone dies. Maybe make
it about the tease, make it about the story again.
Less is more, sometimes.

Indigo: In porn or wrestling?

Trevor: Porn. Well, both. Porn and wrestling are
very similar in some ways. I think Harmony had a
real point earlier – she might not have realised it –
when she was saying about people thinking they're
watching something they shouldn't be. Backroom
casting, cream-pies, even cum shots in the eye.
Nearly all the time, the girls are completely in
control. I think the thing that pissed me off about
Mark Man is – on that first shoot – he didn't tell
people what was going to happen. I've worked with
Candy Cane – well, I've worked with two or three
of the many Candy Canes in the business – and,
let's be honest, she's not the brightest girl in the
world. She had no idea what was going on. She
was actually scared, and that's not fair.

Indigo: Do you think he did it to get a reaction?

Trevor: I used to think so, but, having spoken to
him since, I think he did it because he isn't a
professional. I've seen guys get dragged off set and
beaten up for less than that, you know?

Indigo: You've seen that?

Trevor: A few times. If you're really intent on trying something new in porn, in moving things forward, I think you've got to be smart about it. You need to present something in a way that makes the audience not even think to doubt it. Cream pie surprises are ludicrously badly acted, "rape" scenes are a waste of time because there is a camera in the room and – if you're committing a rape – why would you incriminate yourself? Shit, there's usually a camera in place to document the "abduction" and subsequent car journey.

Indigo: It ruins credibility.

Trevor: Destroys it, and pulls you out of the scene. At least with an old-school honest fuck scene, you don't misinterpret it: it's two people fucking in front of cameras.

Indigo: So, say porn calms down for a few years, downplays itself. What would be an example of something that porn could do, new and different, to reinvigorate the medium?

Trevor: I don't know. If I knew that, I'd do it. Or maybe sell it to Mark Man.

He laughs. We all do.

Trevor: We won't know until it happens, and if it's really strong, we won't recognise it straight away.

Indigo: How do you mean?

Trevor: Okay, here's an example. Did you ever hear of the third biggest wrestling company?

Indigo: No.

Trevor: Yeah, they were good, there was this one guy who I really liked, but he never broke the mainstream the way some wrestlers do. He did one of the smartest things I've ever seen, at a time when wrestling was changing. He worked for a small upstart company, a little outfit in Philadelphia who dared to go head-to-head with the big two. I never worked there, but I've worked with a lot of guys who did. They were very different. Underground. Hardcore. Extreme. But they could work; they *got* it. They had a very loyal following, of educated fans who knew how the business worked - or at least thought they did, but they never let that stop them appreciating a good match. The one thing they did do, though, was whenever a wrestler tried something unique or difficult and they blew the spot[8] , the crowd would chant: 'You fucked up!'.

Indigo: Isn't that a bit disrespectful?

Trevor: No. I mean, it sounds it, but you had to be there. Sure they could heckle, but they also cheered more when guys got it right – when a spot came

---

[8]messed up with a planned move

together beautifully – than any other fans I've ever seen. To me, they were the best fans in the world; they were switched on. They didn't think the match was two guys trying to win something, having a competition over arbitrary bragging rights, they knew it was a show with some of the finest athletes in the world performing.

Indigo: Didn't that cheapen it?

Trevor: No, not at all. If anything, the fact that these wrestlers had nothing to win or lose, the fact that they would go out there each night and risk their bodies for no other reason than to *entertain*, I think that means more than if a boxer gets knocked out in a legitimate competition.

Indigo: How so?

Trevor: They're not doing it for the glory of a win; they're doing it for the love of the industry. But I digress. This guy – and be damned if I can't remember his name – a Mexican wrestler who had this move where he'd jump to the top rope, balance for a second, and then jump on his opponent. You might call it high risk twenty years ago maybe, but fairly commonplace nowadays. This one time I was watching him, he jumped up, and then lost his balance and fell off the ropes. He managed to tuck his head in time, but he landed on his back in the middle of the ring. The crowd instantly kicked off with the "you fucked up!" chants. They loved it; they were all on their feet.

Indigo: He messed it up?

Trevor: So I thought. Next time I see him, different crowd and different arena. He does it again. Same fall, same response. 'You fucked up!'

Indigo: Bad luck?

Trevor: No. It's a spot. He planned to do it. The crowd loved chanting in unison, and the chant they loved most of all was; "you fucked up!", but they didn't always get a chance unless someone screwed up on a show. This guy, he was giving them a chance to do it. And the crowd didn't even realise. Post-kayfabe[9]. In an industry where people beat the shit out of each other, and risk hurting each other, where the bar is constantly getting raised higher and higher, and in a day and age where no one believes wrestling is genuine sport, he gave the crowd a reason to pop without any risk to anyone, and the crowd thought they were seeing something real, something genuine.

Indigo: He was playing them.

---

[9] Kayfabe = the portrayal of staged events within the wrestling industry as real or true, a code word of sorts for maintaining this reality within the realm of the general public

Trevor: Exactly. Wrestling works best when there is no pretence over the realness, when there is a nod and a wink and a lot of entertainment, but he found a way of doing something different within that framework. At the moment, it takes itself too seriously, tries to be about "competition". Some people like that. Other people want it to return to the old days with a mix of both, but it's a difficult thing to put the genie back in the bottle. I think the porn industry is going to have a similar struggle; everyone is jaded, with entertainment and real life. That's why people these days are desperate to see something they think is real, whether it's in wrestling, porn, or something brand new that we've never heard of before in any medium.

Indigo: You think it should be more about characters?

Trevor: The world is already all about characters. Like I said earlier, people can lose themselves in it. I've seen it a lot, and people try and project that shit onto you as well. But we all get caught up in it, right? That's why I used my character at the beginning, to make an impact in the court. I mean, you know what it's like, right?

Indigo: What do you mean?

Trevor: You're playing a character, as much as anyone else. We all do it. Mark Man is the super-celebrity porn star with mainstream appeal. John is the wounded intellectual. And you're the care-free, barely contained hell-raiser, selling a liberal dose of middle-class anarchy for $7.95 a month to your subscribers. That's the problem with this generation, we don't know who we are any more. The best we can be is a faded reproduction of something that came before us. Warhol's law stated that we'd all get fifteen minutes of fame; the only variable is how long you can make that fifteen minutes last. I mean, look at you; you're Hunter S. Thompson with stabilisers. You sell your safe "gonzo" to the masses. What's your most famous quote? "I'd like to advocate drugs and alcohol, but they've never worked for me."

Indigo: I said that after being arrested for possessing drugs.

Trevor: Yeah, two measly pre-rolled cannabis joints. You probably sit at home burning resin holes in your shirts before you go on TV to talk about living with your "addiction". You'd rebel against anarchy, if there was a dollar in it. If activity became the norm, you'd sell the image of sedentary. You represent counter-counter-culture. Everything we do is for the character. We can't sell our genuine selves because no-one knows who they are anymore, and even if they did, they wouldn't want anyone to see the real them. We can only sell an idea of ourselves, and that becomes our identity.

It's true. If I worked for a tobacco company, I would run triathlons. If I was a dietician, I'd eat junk food all the time. I've been doing this character for years: the clothes, the smoking, the drug use. Even arguing with the "editor". Trevor is the first person to see through it, but if it's good for the goose it's good for the gander.

Indigo: So, you're a bad parody of what you think a wrestler turned porno star should be?

Trevor: Aren't we all bad parodies of what we think humans are supposed to be?

**

Indigo: In your opinion, what do you think the future of porn will be?

Mark Man: (*Smiling*) My ex-wife and I have a few ideas.

**

Indigo: What are you going to do next?

Trevor: Settle down, start a family. I've started seeing Kayleigh. She's got a great little boy; it would be nice to have something like that in my life. I mean, after I lost my junk, I thought family was off the table.

Kayleigh: Yeah, what Trevor said. We've got a good nest-egg for the future, but we never know what's going to happen with Trevor's treatment, and the cancer is still spreading.

Kayleigh has come through into the living room and joined us. She cosies up to Trevor on the sofa and takes his hand. It's a... nice moment.

Indigo: You'll stand by him?

Kayleigh: Always.

**

Indigo: So what's next for John Thomas? (*Haha, this will never get old for me.*)

John: I've no idea. I've got nothing left after the court case.

Indigo: That's not true, is it? Trevor told me that from his end of the settlement, he gave you the original patent back.

John: Yeah, but he kept all the money. That was the important bit.

Indigo: Mark Man made the money on the back of the idea; it didn't come with the money.

John: Yeah, but it's all been done now. No one's going to care anymore. The last few films with coloured jizz haven't done well, even with the publicity from the court case. Who wants to pay to see something they've already seen?

Indigo: So what will you do with the patent?

John: I don't know. Probably nothing.

Indigo: Back in the drawer, huh?

**

Indigo: So, legally speaking, you've come out of this the worst. Mark Man Inc. is no more; you've lost the patent. So what's next?

Mark Man: You know, the money I can live without. We can always make more. I wish we still had the patent, though. It was a real shame, losing that. I have ideas for it. There could be a lot more money to be made out of it, for a lot of people.

Demi: We're already back on our feet.

Indigo: How?

Demi: *Hello* magazine has promised us two million dollars for the exclusive marriage photos. And we're running a competition where the readers can name our second child.

Indigo: You're getting remarried? I thought you only just got divorced? Congratulations.

Demi: We were relative nobodies the first time around. There's good money to be made by remarrying.

This could be the biggest union on the planet. Bigger than Will and Kate, bigger than if Diana had married Dodi Al-Fayed. Bigger than Mario and Sonic at the Olympic Games if it had happened in the 16-bit era.

Mark Man: Yeah, but that's just the start. We've started a bidding war for the conception movie. The winning bidder gets the first full penetration video of Demi and me; the King and Queen of Porn, the First Couple of Fucking. The Beckhams of Bukkaki on Blu-ray.

Demi: And footage of the birth all in one package!

Mark Man: And then we're going to retreat from public life. We can't stay young forever.

Demi: Yeah, we want to retire with some dignity.

**

So there it is: The full story of coloured cumshots. Two court cases, three appeals, one patent and one crazy idea.

When I started this absurd journey, I thought it would be a short one. An article, a curio, a side-column. What I didn't expect was to come out the other side having been taught a lesson in nobility by a cancer-riddled porn star. Trevor Goodenough: truly a modern-day eunuch. If I take one moral away from this whole experience, from now on I will try and be my own man, to report not around the story, not as the story, but with the story.

However, I fear that when I wake up tomorrow, I will write this off as a bad idea, and go back to being the same old not-really-me I've always been. A luxury Trevor Goodenough doesn't have.

And lest it feel that I don't know how to end a book, I want to leave you with this final thought: (pleonastic meditations removed by publisher's request. They have the final say, not me or you – your move, fucko. – Editor)

Fin.

Thanks and honourable mentions

Thanks go first and foremost to my very patient long-term editor Nico Reznick, you make me a better writer. My long-standing partner in crime Nick Calloway for the cover and the adventures. James for the proof-reading, and criticism of my repeat use of commas followed by ands, and other errors. Richard Wyllie-Howkins for the feedback for this and other books. Maziar Shahsafdari for the genuine unbridled enthusiasm for my books, even when I'm all out myself. My training partner Tom Malin for dragging me out of the house at least once a day. To my cats for making the job of sit-at-home writer less lonely.

Most of all, thanks to my old employers at Sweatshop (genuine name for a UK store that sells running shoes which are – allegedly – made in sweat shops), if you hadn't sent me on an expensive two-day training course, explaining how doing what we love makes us great at our jobs, I might never have quit to do something I love.

But even more most-of-all than that, thanks to all my Kickstarter supporters, without whom this book might never have happened (I'm contractually obligated to say that after a crowd-sourcing campaign, but I genuinely mean it; thanks).

GENERIC VAMPIRE NOVEL #937 by C Z Hazard

When cult science fiction novelist Shamus Ohio wrote his latest book, Horrorcaust, he expected it to appease his publishers and earn him a small paycheck. Instead, it re-defined the public perception of the "vampyre" for an entire generation.

With mainstream success, Shamus comes face to face with the real blood-sucking parasite: the media. Everyone wants a piece of Shamus, as the mass hysteria surrounding his novel and the fight for control of his intellectual property threaten to tear his mind and conscience apart.

When fact starts mirroring fiction with deadly results, can the writer be held responsible? Can anyone achieve mainstream popularity without selling their soul? Can any piece of fiction make the leap from one medium to another with its core intact? What exactly is Parma ham, and why do people insist on serving it with rocket? All of these questions and more will be asked, if not answered.

For people who may already dislike vampire fiction, new-media, the film industry, hyperbole, social media, the 24-hour news culture and other day-to-day trappings of post-millennial life.

ANHEDONIA by Nico Reznick

Alex Austin is nearing thirty; a self-confessed fake, charlatan, degenerate and – worst of all – a failed poet, Alex's life has become a meaningless sequence of bad habits and poor decisions. He ekes out a living doing a job that makes him feel dirty and ashamed. His only friend, JB – the developmentally arrested offspring of two famous psychologists – is just as broken as he is.

Incapable of experiencing pleasure or joy without resorting to unhealthy extremes, Alex's days are divided between sofa-mining and grief-surfing; shiftily rummaging down the backs of display model couches for fallen currency, and cynically manipulating strangers' grief for his own depraved gratification.

As his self-destructive behaviour escalates and his self-loathing deepens, Alex is relentlessly, savagely cross-examined and berated by the voice of his own conscience, which speaks to him in the sneering, righteous tones of a retired TV news show host. When Edie – a former grief conquest, now wise to his scam – shows up out of his sordid past, he's not sure if she's here to save him or destroy him, and he can't decide which is the more terrifying prospect.

About the Author

C Z Hazard is or has been a comic shop manager, biomechanical gait analyser, wrestler, DJ, rap artist manager, YouTube "Celebrity", blogger, Guitar Hero legend-in-his-own-lunchtime, award-winning toy customiser, comic book writer, champion of the Oxford comma, a lifetime science fiction fan, and Time Magazine Man of the Year 2006 (look it up!).

Now I write, and get confused whether I'm supposed to be doing this section in first or third person.

I share a house with two cats, my editor, and far too many plastic toy robots.

Other books may happen.

Follow me at:

www.facebook.com/CZHZRD

@CZHAZARD on Twitter

46802289R00096

Made in the USA
Charleston, SC
25 September 2015